The Last Story

They say you can feel death in a room but it's not true ... Ken Tiger is there on the bed. Eyes closed, arms crossed neatly over his chest. It's as if he knew this was coming. I stand at the end of the bed, staring down at him as if I'd come to look in on a sleeping child.

I wonder how different his life would have been if Ada could have loved him in the way that he loved her, if her eyes hadn't always been fixed on some other place. A homeland, a dream. What if, licking the sticky crumbs of lotus cake from her fingers, she had told him that she would come away with him. I don't know.

All I know is the story I have.

Shortlisted, *The Australian/* Vogel Literary Award, 2004
Winner, TAG Hungerford Award, 2006
Shortlisted, Barbara Jefferis Award for Literature, 2009
Winner, *Sydney Morning Herald* Best Novelist of the Year, 2009

In this rich and evocative novel, Nelson moves her narrative easily between Perth and China, between the past and the future, juxtaposing the inner life of her protagonist, Maya Wise, with the political upheaval of the Hong Kong handover. The themes of exile and dislocation are cleverly drawn and Maya's imagined wanderings into wartime Shanghai give her refuge in someone else's past. The language displays great restraint as well as a real lyrical beauty. – Sydney Morning Herald, Judge's Report

This book contains book club discussion questions. For a full version of the Book Club notes, including an interview with the author, please visit http://www.fremantlepress.com.au.

The Last Sky

ALICE NELSON

FREMANTLE
PRESS
fine independent publishing

First published 2008 by
FREMANTLE PRESS
25 Quarry Street, Fremantle
(PO Box 158, North Fremantle 6159)
Western Australia.
www.fremantlepress.com.au

2nd edition published 2010.

Consultant editor Janet Blagg
Cover designer Tracey Gibbs
Cover images: Robert Churchill, Eva Serrabassa
Printed by Everbest Printing Company, China

Papers used by Fremantle Press are natural, recyclable
products made from wood grown in sustainable forests;
the manufacturing processes conform to the environmental
regulations of the country of origin.

National Library of Australia
Cataloguing-in-publication data

Nelson, Alice, 1980–
The last sky / Alice Nelson
2nd ed.
9781921361920 (pbk).

A823.4

Publication of this title was assisted by the Commonwealth
Government through the Australia Council, its arts funding and
advisory body.

for
Brenda Walker

We live permanently in the recurrence
of our own stories, whatever story we tell.
Michael Ondaatje

My husband told me a story about buildings before we came here. In the central district the old Hongkong and Shanghai Bank looms proudly above the other buildings, full of British bankers and rich Americans. When the People's Bank of China built their rival headquarters several blocks away they designed the top of the tower to look like a knife's edge thrusting towards the British bank. It was no accident, Joseph laughed. In Hong Kong nothing was left to simmer under the surface.

It must have been during those first December days that he told me the story, before he got caught up in the suspended time of the interior. Perhaps on one of the days we walked together up a mountain path and saw the vista of islands rising up from the China Sea, curving smoothly out of the green glassiness like the contours of a body, the mist of early morning a canopy against the blue of the sky. We looked at one another, each about to say something, our double gasp of awe fading in the air.

It was these luminous moments, rescued from days of waiting and silence, that I was trying to hold on to.

I had never seen real flamingoes until I came to the Kowloon Gardens in Hong Kong. On the lake there is an island pink with them. You can sit on the benches and watch them standing still and straight in the reeds. There are green tortoises too, which tip the surface of the water, and great orange coi. Businessmen in suits mill around the edge of the lake, smoking sweet clove cigarettes and squinting into the sun. Beyond the lake there is an aviary where murmured conversations are held under the squalling of white cockatoos and galahs.

Walk out of the gardens past the White Mosque and the Mirimar Shopping Arcade and you come to Kowloon Square where fountains send drifts of spray onto grimy tables. There are noodlehouses and fruit shops selling bruised mangosteens, and jackfruit that smell rancid when you break them open. Grey apartment towers lean over the square and sometimes you can see laundry flapping from bamboo poles on the balconies.

On the south side of the square, next to the Go-Go

Club, is the Sun Hing Lung Medicine Company. Here you can buy cream made from crushed black pearls to smooth away wrinkles, and Japan Wonderful Oil to improve the constitution. In summer they sell Pa Po Tang Seal pills and Red Flower Oil to stop heat rash and in winter there are Golden Gun capsules to warm up the blood. In a room behind a blue curtain old Mr Lung mixes cures and potions and sells sex tonics and prophylactics to girls and businessmen.

We live at the university. The flat comes with Joseph's position. There are a dozen of us in the residents' apartments, all living in spaces carved out of what must once have been a grand old house. Inches behind the head of our bed is someone else's shower and at night I can hear the water dripping slowly, drop by drop. The halls smell of ginseng and dried fish. I hear cooking noises and washing noises so I know there must be other people living here, but I never see them. I saw a hand once, reaching out of a window to catch a dust fairy.

After Joseph leaves in the mornings I wander through the apartment, staring out the windows. The glass is old and disillusioned; it warps the surfaces of things. It's not a home, this place. Some of our things are still in the boxes they were shipped in. The Mexican plates are carefully wrapped in newspaper at the bottom of a crate. There is a formica table littered with Joseph's books and papers, all of them written in the strange box-like characters of his second language. I stare at them, the shapes and lines that I know are letters, but the eye skips uneasily. They defend their secrets, geometrically.

I lean against the counter as I wait for the kettle to boil, for the hot cloud of steam from a glazed cup. Joseph brings me packets of tea leaves from oasis towns in the desert. The same brews, he says, the desert people have been drinking for thousands of years. The tribes of the Taklamakan Desert and the salt flats of Lop Nor, a vast shimmering mirage of the lake that was once there. He tells me about their abandoned villages. The slender trunks of desiccated fruit trees and the corner posts of dwellings. There are lintels and doorways and beams falling across each other, with the mark of the carpenter's adze still clearly on them. Shards of pottery, scraps of leather.

I walk down the stairs and into the sunlight. At noon the courtyard is deserted, the students gone to the cafeteria or the street food stalls. There's a stone bench by a small pond. I like to sit against the coolness of stone with the smell of damp, dark air rising up from the pond, my bare feet tucked up under my skirt. Everything is still. Joseph has told me about the famous water gardens of China, the canals and fountains carved out of men's imaginations, this desire for stillness at the hearts of cities.

There are things I could do here in Hong Kong. I could

teach English at one of the private language schools. I could befriend some of the other expatriate wives and we could meet for lunch at the Hong Kong Club and shop for Chinese silk at the markets in Repulse Bay. I could learn to play mahjong.

The women in the square play mahjong. They call it swimming without water. The sweeping movements of the arms across the table look like the movement of flesh through water.

Joseph is always tired when he comes home in the evenings. I see him in the doorway, a tall man in a pale coat running his hands through his hair. In my dreams I find a way to make his arms remember their desire, but when I wake he is the same silhouette of a man, sighing as he turns in his sleep.

He sits there in silence, balancing a glass of gin on the arm of the chair. He is a man who has never become accustomed to the slow, quiet ways of domestic life, never wanted the smell of soap and pine needles and stew bubbling on the stove in winter and the bother of possessions. China, and the lost cultures of its deserts, was always among us. He is a man who slips away on expeditions into the desert and returns suntanned and exhausted, unused to the ways of cities.

I sit at the table with my new pen and a clean page before me. My head aches, the light shines through the glass.

Last week I saw a man buy a nightingale. It was near the souk-like shops on Hong Kong Island. In the mornings the lane markets are crowded and noisy and the dipping awnings create a false twilight. It is a world of alleys and dim passages. Take a wrong turn, which is easy to do, and you find yourself staring into the doorway of somebody's house, six sets of dark eyes returning your gaze.

The Chinese love birds. Few apartments are without at least one songbird. They hang in intricate cages made from fine bamboo. Perhaps they love the quiet swish of trapped wings, the flare of colour, the high notes of song.

In the markets the lane they call Bird Street rings with the chatter of a thousand birds. The cages sway with movement, one hanging from another. The air is slightly fetid and thick with the dusty flutter of contained feathers.

A Chinese man is pointing to a nightingale. He is old, his face is lined and dark, but his hair is thick and black. He stares at the nightingale tenderly, almost lovingly, and hands over a thick pile of notes. I don't know how much it costs to buy a nightingale.

Holding the cage high, he walks away down the lane. Passing a row of electronic stalls, blazing with neon and noisy with computer games and gadgets, he looks like a kind of allegory. Like a tender story from another time.

He walks away from the markets and I find myself following him. I want to know where he is going, see where he is off to. It is just a bit of fun, I tell myself, a little holiday from reality. So I clutch my shopping bag to my chest and pick my way through the swarms of locals and tourists.

It is easy enough to keep him in sight. I fix my eyes on his bobbing dark head as he strides purposefully along the edge of the sidewalk, weaving his way past all the peddlers and the sleepy-eyed men standing outside their shops. Sometimes I lose him, only to see the rattan cage again in the middle of the throng waiting at the traffic light.

A bicycle cuts in front of me and I jump back, my heart suddenly pounding, my hands shaking. The man with the bird is nowhere in sight.

I stand in the square. The sun is misty, the sun of the hot season. People look at me. People will still look at a white woman here. You don't have to wear silk stockings to be a lady in the colonies any more, but people still look at you with curiosity and an old, muted hostility.

Then suddenly I see him again. He steps out of a teahouse, still holding the cage, and stands looking across the square for a moment before he turns and heads north.

We walk all the way to the Convention Centre by the harbour. It's a spring afternoon, a Saturday, and the harbour is full of brides. I count seven Chinese girls in full tulle skirts smiling anxiously into cameras on the steps of the centre. The pastel skyline of the island is a good backdrop for wedding photographs and on spring weekends you have to weave your way through bridal parties. The brides' smiles stretch across their faces and they move daintily and coyly but I cannot believe that they are all as serene as they appear. One of the brides, a young girl with gold at her throat and ears, turns to snap at a clumsy flowergirl with a foot on her frothy skirts. For an unphotographed, unnoticed moment her eyes are hard and her voice is sharp before she turns back to the camera and smiles again.

I lose him for a minute and then I find him again, leaning against the Clock Tower and lighting a cigarette. The Clock Tower, tall and brick and British as bulldogs, is one of the more picturesque remnants of a different time. It sits staunchly there on the harbour by the ferry terminals and every time I pass it I can't help thinking of tea and sponge cake and sweeping skirts. I find a low bench nearby and sit, watching the outline of his face, just the cheekbones and the swell of the lips.

Sometimes I watch the lines of Joseph's face like this when he turns away from me in bed at night.

The nightingale man flicks away his cigarette and, holding the cage high, walks away from the harbour, from the late afternoon haze and the ferries rubbing their sides against the docks. I slowly uncross my legs and follow him, falling back far enough for him not to be able to hear the tread of my feet.

He picks up the pace now, turning abruptly down a side street and holding the cage closer to him. He walks bent slightly forward, like someone leaning into a wind. I look down at my feet, at the sidewalk, trying to fit just one step into each square before the crack. We weave around corners and down other streets I don't recognise. I begin to grow nervous, I don't know this area, we are far now from where I live and it will be dark soon. The evenings are thick and warm here but the shadows fall quickly.

Perhaps I should not have come, perhaps I should have turned away, fallen back, stayed sitting in the sun by the harbour.

We walk on, up some steps to a low bridge. Suddenly, in the middle of the bridge, he stops short and turns to face me. I wait for the accusation, the question, but he says nothing, just stands there staring me straight in the eye. I stand there, clutching my hands around my elbows, feeling foolish, trying to think of some excuse, some explanation. He must have known all along, yet I never saw him glance back. He is still standing there, looking patiently at me. I open my mouth to say something, but nothing comes out. Unnerved, I uncross my arms, turn around down the steps and walk away, back the way I thought I had come, towards home, towards my husband.

When I first came to Hong Kong I saw that I had not even begun to imagine it as it really was. On that first morning six months ago, across the dark water, I saw the lights of an enormous city glowing. Joseph's Hong Kong, a royal white city built on a rock. Hong Kong, a string of islands, silent in the haze, rising up from the dim blue coast of China.

We came by ship from China. 'It's the best way,' Joseph said, standing beside me on the deck, his arm lightly around my shoulders. 'You have to look closely. It's a city that only reveals itself in details. There's no straightforward beauty. Not like an Australian city.'

I held up my hand to shade my eyes from the sun. This was a new world he was showing me.

The night before, our last night in Perth, he had started awake violently, calling out something before lying back against the pillow with his eyes wide open. I slipped my arm across his chest.

'Nightmare?'

'Mmmm. Don't worry.'

I brought him a glass of water and watched as he drank in the darkness, his throat contracting with each gulp.

I slid close to him and placed my head on his chest, feeling the brace of bone and the thump of his heart. We lay in each other's arms with the light from the moon on us until he moved almost imperceptibly, signalling that he wanted to turn over, wanted to sleep free from hot limbs and awkward weight. He has never been a man who can spend a whole night in someone's arms.

On the ship there was only the pulse of the engines, the swish of the wind and the faraway lights of the villages that line the estuary. They slipped by, faint and distant, as the river broadened towards the sea. And then, after the long hours of the night, after the thick white mists of the open sea, the fog lifted like a curtain and there was another harbour. A harbour full of ships, hundreds of ships floating motionless in the thick whiteness of the dawn. One by one they loomed out of the darkness, shapeless freighters with foreign flags above their sterns hanging in the clammy breeze, the layered ferry boats, the junks and sampans cluttered between them.

And then, like another flotilla, the buildings. Rising up from the mist, pressing upon each other, immense and clean. White, silver and shimmering gold with masses of windows like portholes on a ship. The jagged rooflines, the glimmering towers and peaks, and beyond them all the looming greenness of the mountains, the still white villas and winding roads.

Sometimes I can't trust my memories of the city, the physical truth of them. I walk through the city every day, gaze out at it, live in a high room above it, but it becomes for me the point around which stories and memories coalesce. It is a world half-invented out of memory and desire.

In those first days, I watched Hong Kong as one watches a silent film, the roar of the city soundless beyond thick glass. From the stillness of the hotel room I watched the rise and fall of skyscrapers, the jets gliding through the television aerials, flashes of sun on windows, the Nine Hills of Kowloon looming through the shimmer of heat. I looked for the bank built like the slice of a knife.

And the street. If I pressed my forehead against the cool glass and looked down, it was there, in all its seething, silent motion. The clamorous shop fronts, the gilded dragons, the swarming crowds, the hawkers' carts, the wavering bicycles. And always the cranes swinging, jackhammers drilling, the groups of men in hard hats poring over plans. A city like a story, always under construction, buildings torn down and replaced with ruthless speed. Bamboo scaffolding folding like delicate cages around the skyscrapers. The skyline changing every month, like a work in progress, like a forest.

In those first mornings I lay in the deep, gleaming hotel bath. It was big enough to float in and the enamel was so smooth that you slipped beneath the water if you didn't hold yourself up. You could quickly find the waterline rising above your chin, the firm warmth pressing against your eyelids. There's an iron bathtub in my mother's house, with real claw feet and the old kind of enamel. Sometimes she would sit on the edge of the tub and talk to me. Not often, she's not a woman for idle chat.

There's no-one to sit on the edge of a bathtub here. Joseph sits in a dark room surrounded by maps and books. His office at the university looks like a base camp. One whole wall is taken up by a map of the Taklamakan Desert. Joseph's desert. On the map, marked in red, are the expeditions that have criss-crossed the desert. Stein 1985. Stein 1988. Stein-Wise 1992. Clean, sweeping lines that tell nothing of the billowing heat, the air so hot it burns the lungs. The dust storms, the false turns, the endless dunes, the toll on the body.

I remember when Joseph would stumble back to me out of the desert. Exhausted, like an animal that has found its way home. His head in my lap, my hair long enough to spread over his face. His hand sweeping out, touching the side of my face.

On nights when it was too hot to sleep he took me travelling through his desert. In the Sand Sea the dunes pile up like tidal waves and great ribs of rock lie in lines like ships frozen at anchor. He speaks about the desert as if he was reciting a poem. 'No words can properly describe the beauty of those sweeping curves of sand. They have to be seen. In the early morning or late evening when the hills throw cool dark shadows. The world ends out there.'

The desert is a place of danger. At nights the temperatures drop below zero and there are winds laden with knife-edged particles of ice. And the winds of the day with their driving grains that sting your face and legs like needles. False oases shimmer like distant lakes but are really dry expanses of salt.

But what fascinates him is the buried history of the desert. The lost worlds of ten thousand years ago when the climate was kinder and men lived there, hunting and keeping cattle, and acacia trees grew in plains of sand. Pomegranates, fruit trees, villages with temples and wells. Trade routes and enmities, gods and kings.

He tells me about the desert storms. The infamous spring storms, which are called black storms. They come from nowhere, the sky suddenly grows dark, the sun becomes a dark red ball of fire behind a thickening veil of dust. There is a fierce hissing and lashing sand and pebbles. The roar and howl of the storm can last for hours. The men wrap themselves in felts and wait out the violence, huddled against the sides of cars. I see him there, safe, encased in softness in the eye of the storm.

It was the desert that brought us to Hong Kong. For years, perhaps since before I met him, Joseph had been looking for ways to get back to the desert. In many ways he was a man living in the wrong world. He belonged to a time in history where high-born men spent their inheritances organising expeditions into jungles and deserts. But he had no inheritance, and there were no more benevolent Royal Societies to send clutches of explorers off to the vast and silent reaches of the world. The world was no longer dignified and leisurely and he had to scramble along with the rest of us for travel grants and research fellowships.

The posting here was a stroke of luck, as they say. Joseph's mentor, the great sinologist Aurel Stein, had landed a senior position at Hong Kong University and he had helped smooth the way for Joseph. To head up a research team and write a series of reports on the history of the northern desert. The university had money and Stein had vouched for his protégé.

'We're onto a good thing,' Joseph said to me excitedly. 'A pay rise and free housing. We'll rent out the house here. You can apply for leave. Write. We'll be all right for money.'

He knelt in front of me and slipped his hands under the sleeves of my shirt and cupped them around my shoulders. His open palms were smooth and warm. His face was so close to mine I could no longer see his features, only his curling hair against my skin. 'Say yes,' he whispered.

Three months later I found myself in a hotel room above the street in a Chinese city, my husband already packing for a month-long trip to the desert.

I sat and watched my face in the darkness of the glass and below, the whole city cast into a neon glare. The vast collage of fluorescent signs, their Chinese characters marching one behind each other all the way up to the mountains. All the neon signs are obliged by law to be motionless, Joseph told me, to avoid confusing the navigators of aircraft. And so they stand silent and unblinking. There is something unnerving about the huge, unwavering stillness of them.

In the hotel room I sat on the edge of the bed, leaning slightly forward so I wouldn't tip back into the sinking softness of the mattress. I looked down at my shoes, which were soft leather, made to look like ballet slippers. Wrong for this city. The first morning on the streets they were streaked with dirt and grime.

Three days after we arrived Joseph left on his first field trip. He bent down to kiss me but I could tell that he was already gone, his eye on the desert. He left me, my husband, to the wide empty evenings and the muted stillness of the hotel. To the city. '*Welcome to Hong Kong,*' one of the brochures says, '*the Last Crown Colony.*'

Who can best tell the strange history of the island? The sepia soldiers in British scarlet, their great ships furrowing the seas, the brass of their telescopes glinting against the milky blur of the Chinese sky? Or the unsmiling emperors in their palaces, safe behind so much fine gilt and vases blooming with delicate flowers? The broadfaced fishermen, their salt-stiff hands casting the fine lines of their nets against the darkening horizon?

Over it all hangs not the yellow patina of the past, but the slow, dim haze of opium. The forgetfulness of ether. An island, borrowed or stolen, depending on who is telling the story.

The story is the story of any colony. The men in their ships, in imagining a paradise, saw a paradise lost, and so one for the taking. It is written in all the books, again and again, the same story. Only the ending has not been crafted yet and it looms, vague and uncertain on the milky horizon. It is everywhere, the talk of June thirtieth, the Handover, the return of the island to its true owners. It seems to me a strange thing, to borrow a place and then to return it.

In the paper there is an interview with the commander of the British Forces. I can see him in his barracks, the shine of leather and brass, the clean fold of cloth. A man, firm and resolute against a misty Chinese sky, speaking of the duties of Britain, the responsibilities of empire.

'We cannot just throw the key over the border at midnight to the People's Liberation Army and say: "Carry on."'

I imagine a set of keys, glinting brass-bright in the darkness. Tossed, circling, arcing against the huge night.

I can rescue these things from oblivion, make the island some last testament to the meaning of empire, but in the end they will be forgotten and I will be alone with them.

I woke early on those first mornings in the hotel room. If I were at home I would be out of bed immediately, coffee made and at work by eight. But those mornings I lay in bed for a long time, staring up at the ceiling. The room felt too vast. I wanted a narrow bed, a low window.

In the afternoons I walked up to Victoria Peak, the colony's hill station. After the spring rains the road is deserted and everything shines with moisture. The wax trees, the bowers of jasmine and wild indigo, the wavering butterflies, the birds scattering before me. The villas lie half-hidden in shrubberies, their names shining from brass plates. *Cloudlands. The Eyrie. Strawberry Hill.* And suddenly, through a frame of trees, the vista of the city. The sea, blue-green, island-studded. The pale skyscrapers of Kowloon, sleek and sun-struck, the ferries making lines across the harbour, the jetfoil streaming across the water. The city is elsewhere, the huge endless stir of it is far from me.

These will be the things that I will save from oblivion: a young Chinese man stepping out of a pink Rolls Royce, the ceaseless clatter of the streets, the name *Cloudlands,* the pungent smell of ginger and the vision of a hundred islands rising out of a huge green sea.

I'm out tramping through the city, staring at the windows of shops or up at the sun glancing off the buildings. In the early morning, before the heat has settled over the city, you can still smell the faint scent of orchids mixed with the dust from the roads and the cool air drifting from the mountains.

Standing on the edge of the square I see the nightingale man again, the one I followed last week. Sitting at a table outside a shop with a cup in his hands, he turns his head to look at me. Yes, it's him, the same large eyes, the same slightly hunched shoulders. There's a hesitance in his look, a quietness.

Feeling I need to make some sort of gesture, I move forward to say something. He looks steadily at me as I approach.

'Hello. I followed you the other day. I'm sorry. I don't know why. The bird …'

The nightingale, he told me many months later, was precious to him because when he was a boy his mother had always kept one in the house. She sang too, her voice echoing the swerves and trills of the bird's.

He takes a sip of tea. 'You did not stay to say hello.'

'No.'

'You are the wife of the archaeologist.'

I nod. I should not be surprised. Hong Kong is a city of undercurrents where everything is known and mysterious at once.

'My name is Ken Tiger.'

'You speak English very well.' *Never trust them when they can speak English better than you*, a red-faced American had laughed once to me over a dinner table.

'Yes. I am good at languages. English, French, Russian.' There's no boasting in his voice. He smiles at me. 'Would you like some tea? This is my shop here.' He gestures behind him.

The front room of the shop is crowded with plywood shelves full of books. They are mostly Chinese books but I can see a few piles of English novels, some poetry. I follow him through a fringe of bamboo beads into the back of the shop.

The room is dim and dry. Everything fits, or is wedged, between stacks of books. The nightingale is there, hanging from the ceiling in its bamboo cage.

There are strange obsessions in people. I met a couple once who collected antique pianos in the same way that other people collect stamps or spoons. They found them all over the world, these pianos, and shipped them home and mended them lovingly. Their house was full of pianos; they lined the walls of every room. In the bedroom there was a huge grand piano pushed up close to their bed. It was an old German model, the husband told me excitedly, the kind of piano that Beethoven would have played. He played a few notes for me. The whole house quivered faintly.

But no, leave the house with the pianos, leave it for another story. I am here, in a room with bamboo blinds and musty incense with a Chinese man and a nightingale.

He selects, from drawers full of tea, a tiny pouch and empties the tea leaves into his palm.

'See,' he says slowly, stretching out his hand to me, 'how the leaves are not broken but dried into tiny buds. An Oolong.'

I sniff the tea and look up at him, not sure what I am supposed to gain from the scent.

'It is about all of the senses, the Chinese tea ceremony, not just the taste.'

He raises the tea to his nose, breathing deeply and closing his eyes as the fine, sharp scent rises from the leaves. I watch his old, smooth face and the dark lines of his eyebrows. It is a ritual, scent for the sake of scent. I can understand. Many times I have lifted a hot mug to my face, letting the steam moisten my nose and lips.

He takes a tiny teapot from a cabinet against the wall. It is round and squat, like a nectarine, and the colour of the clay that lines the riverbanks in the south of Australia.

'It's made of clay, no?'

'Yes. Red sand clay. You have to dig very deep to find this kind of clay.'

He wraps his hands around the teapot. 'It is all built by hand, a pot like this. Not shaped on a wheel. And there is no glaze. To seal the inside you boil old tea leaves with water for three hours. The oils in the tea seal the pores in the clay.'

He separates a small handful of tea with fine chopsticks and places it in the pot, pouring the boiling water swiftly over it. He covers the teapot and as it steeps he lines up two cups. They are small and narrow, like spools of thread.

'The mistake people make,' he says, uncovering the teapot, 'is to let the tea steep for too long. You must learn when to pour.'

In smooth arcs he pours the tea into the cups, not pouring one cup at a time, but moving the pot around over the cups so that they fill together. Back home, in the dark bars of the city, I have seen bartenders pour shots of whisky like this, the alcohol slopping onto the counter.

But this man doesn't spill anything. He passes me a narrow cup, watching closely as I raise it to my lips.

We talk, words drift, layer upon layer. He has read Keats, Shelley, Byron. He likes the novels of Charles Dickens. He likes a good story well told, he says. I tell him that I love to read too.

'Love stories?'

'Yes, I suppose love stories. All kinds. They're all mostly love stories in the end, aren't they?'

Ken Tiger stirs his tea with a spoon that looks like a sliver of bone. In the corner the nightingale quivers its wings. Nightingales are very ordinary-looking birds, despite their legendary voices. They are small, with neat brown feathers. The noise of the square comes in from outside.

'Once all of Hong Kong knew my story,' he says suddenly.

'How did they know?'

'In the same way they know your story, everyone's story.'

'Yes. They certainly devour news of any scandal here, don't they?'

'Devour.' He tests the word out. For a moment he looks like any small boy with a secret.

I watch the dusty light falling in shafts through the window. It falls across my legs and makes patches on the floor. There have been days this summer when I have sat and watched the light until my eyes ached and my head was thick and heavy.

He takes one of the books from a shelf above the desk and opens it. Pressed between the pages are the fragments of a flower, paper-thin and crumbling, a purple skeleton staining the pages of the book.

'An orchid,' he says. 'Once she unpinned the orchid from her dress and placed it in one of my books. I can think of her for hours and yet it is always that moment I come back to.' He stares at the outline of the petals.

'She was like you a little,' he says. 'Something in the eyes, in the set of the eyes. Her name was Ada Lang. Then Ada Kadoorie. And mine was not Ken Tiger then. She was Jewish, from Russia. She came with the Jews who escaped to Shanghai. There were thousands of them. Did you know that? Thousands.'

I had not known. I close my eyes. I want the story, as accurate as a slide rule. As fresh as the smell of fennel.

Somewhere there is an album made up of photographs of Joseph and me. It's a kind of time-lapse progression of our marriage, from our first smiling poses and happy glances to a different, truer kind of landscape.

When I first met Joseph he had no photographs of himself. No childhood snaps or rosy-cheeked portraits to put in a silver frame on the piano. I could only imagine him as a dreamy, thin-faced child.

When we moved into the house by the sea, I used to herd him into the garden and make him sit at the table under the Cape lilac, or stand by the newly planted rose bushes. He was more pliable then, or perhaps happier to please me, and he would stand in the afternoon sun, smiling obligingly.

'You have such a mania for preservation Maya,' he said to me once as I stared at him through the barrel of the camera.

Sometimes I would set the timer and dash into the photo. I look slightly flustered in these shots, always caught brushing my hair back or straightening my skirt.

I don't know why I needed this evolving portrait, this careful, light-caught tabling of the past. When the photographs were developed I would stare at them for hours, trying to decide what they betrayed or revealed about us.

Sitting by the window, a foreigner, alone, staring out at the darkening courtyard, I wish I had brought the photographs with me. I need something to remind me that there is another life apart from this displaced, insubstantial one. The apartment is filled with the noise of Hong Kong traffic: cars accelerating, honks, bicycle bells, sirens.

There was another time when it was not like this. Once we had a real house, friends, a sense of the smooth, round word *future*. The house was on the bay and all the floors sloped south. There were magpies and purple bougainvillea and warm cedar boards. There were blue dishes from Mexico and a path down to the beach.

I write about this house in stories. There is plenty to tell. Here is the bed where I lie with my husband late into the mornings. Here is a man holding his wife, his fingers spread against the small of her back, his eyes cloudy with desire. But the image is hazy already, like a photograph where the shutter has been released too slowly.

At the rattle of the key in the lock, my heart skips foolishly. Dropping his briefcase on the table, Joseph walks slowly into the small living room.

'How's the lady of leisure?'

'Reading poetry.'

He looks at the cover of the book on my lap and turns his head to show a small, strained smile. 'You and your Russians,' he says, backing into a chair and resting his brogues on the coffee table.

'I wanted to read you something.' I flick through the pages. 'Here. There's this beautiful part where he says that when he thinks of Russia it's not the continental mass, not the actual area of the earth's surface. It's a sound "such as you hear in a sea breaking along a shore."'

I look up at him. Since I first met Joseph, I've hoarded things I've come across in my reading to tell him. Anecdotes, pithy or beautiful quotes, matters or events which moved me. I would offer up my fragments, partly to entertain him, but also as a way to fasten down what I most felt and believed. For a long time I have thought about writing a book about the places where art and life intersect. There would be stories, and fragments of stories, in a kind of cultural anthology of the century. I would have to be very careful, Joseph said, not to sound tremendously pretentious.

Give me a pencil and I will draw you a room in a city on the Australian coast. A high room above the sea, a man and a woman. A time when I loved him simply, wrenchingly.

'Let me tell you about Gaugin,' I say. Sunlight pours into the room and Joseph smiles at me.

'Gaugin. The wild man. The island dweller. All those gorgeous women. Yes, tell me.'

He closes his eyes as I'm talking. He looks as if he's asleep but I can tell he's listening.

'At the end of his life he was on one of his islands somewhere. It was a miserable existence at the end. He was totally alone. No beautiful women, just a hut he had built for himself in the jungle. It was squalid and sweltering and he had no idea if his paintings would even be remembered. He was dying but he kept painting, kept dragging himself up from his bed to paint a few more strokes. There wasn't any food and he didn't have the strength to get fresh water. On the lintel above the door of his hut he had carved the phrase, "Be in love and you will always be happy."'

I bend down above him and kiss his lips lightly. He seizes my arms and draws me close to him. I can taste the faint saltiness of his skin. On his lips is the taste of the sea.

But now, years later in a strange country, he is regarding me with a look of faint impatience.

'It's quite lovely don't you think? The idea of Russia being a sound that his people brought with them.'

'I think,' he says, shaking his head, 'that you've become hopelessly sentimental.'

I don't know how we've fallen into this pattern. I inflate and instead of indulging me as he used to, he produces the pin. I stare at him. He has been my husband for six years and I can't think of a single thing to say to him.

I came to Hong Kong in the thirty-second year of my life to accompany my husband and to write a book on the life and work of Nicolas Poussin. It was supposed to be a quiet and productive time for me. A sabbatical from preparing lectures and marking papers and all the demands of my professional life. Without the endless committees and appointments and theses to supervise I would be free to work uninterrupted on Poussin. The extended study that was supposed to follow my doctoral work on French seventeenth-century painting.

These are the things I told the university when I arranged for a hasty leave of absence to come here.

But the truth of it is that I am uncertain, even now, about what made me fall upon this path and choose it as my vocation. I had discovered Poussin while I was studying at the University of New England. After school most young people drifted down to Sydney, to the sandstone university or to the cafes and bars by the quay, but I stayed on in the north. I loved the landscape, the cleanness of its lines, its bareness. And my mother was alone on the farm. My brothers disappeared into the city a long time ago.

On Friday afternoons I would drive out of Armidale to the farm, arriving in the darkness. Sometimes the bottom dam would still hold the reflection of a tiny streak of light. My mother and I would sit and eat dinner across from each other, our reflections pale smears in the dark mirrors of the windows, the fire cracking and shifting behind us.

She would tell me things about the farm: the rabbits' tunnels she had found in the dam wall, the drainage channels she was going to dig beside the track, the rats' nest she had cleared out from behind the fuel stove. Then she would ask about my studies, nodding severely as I spoke. She was a country woman, precise and laconic; it was hard for her to understand the endless sprawl of words wasted on essays and papers about painting and poems.

Once I overheard Joseph talking to someone about my childhood. 'The mother brought them up pretty hard I suspect,' he said. I don't know if he was right.

After dinner we would sit in the armchairs by the fire. My

mother would always have some sewing or knitting in her hands, her needles eating up yards of sturdy wool, the dogs asleep at her feet. I would bring out the books I had brought down from university, tucking my feet up under my knees and balancing a cup of tea on the arm of the chair. We could sit for hours in silence like that, the only sounds the reedy notes of the frogs or the spatter of rain against the roof. Sometimes we would hear shots and their echoes bounding across the cold ridges.

It was by the fire in my mother's house that I saw for the first time Poussin's *Cephalus and Aurora*. The painting shows Cephalus rejecting Aurora, goddess of Dawn. I had read the story in Ovid, but in Poussin's painting an angel holds up a portrait of Cephalus's wife, Procris. It is the portrait that lures him away from Aurora. Poussin knew that a memento, a sign of absence, can make a lost person present and so reinforce memory, strengthen love. Years later, when he was in exile in Italy, he sent his own portrait back to France.

There was no portrait of my father in that house. Only my eldest brother could remember him as someone real, someone who had lived among us. For the rest of us he was a ghost, a name that caused our mother's lips to tighten. Once I asked her about him and she simply raised her palm into the air and walked away from the table. It was as if he had in some way consumed and exhausted her. I don't know what she was like before the great fracture in her life that was his leaving, if she still had the same sense of withholding. Sometimes I think she is like Marthe, the woman in the bath in so many of Bonnard's paintings who is always turning slightly away. She was an efficient mother and she spent hours sewing our clothes, chopping wood to heat our baths and cooking for us, but there was always an insistence on her right to her own self and her own thoughts. A refusal to subsume herself in us.

It wasn't until many years later that I wondered if perhaps it was this unyielding self-containment that had driven my father away.

During those university years, and later when I moved west for my doctoral studies, I was desperately trying to force my way into the world of ideas, to forge the kind of mind that could contemplate the abstract. I travelled to France to study for a semester, I wrote assiduously researched papers, I won a scholarship to the University of Western Australia to study under an expert in early French painting. But my mind kept veering back to the specific, the peripheral, the places where art meets life. I would try to contemplate the spatial planes in Poussin's self-portraits and find myself instead thinking about the particular hesitance in his gaze or wondering what his relationship was to the woman with the crown in the background.

In Hong Kong I sit with my boxes full of notes, staring at all the archival material I've photocopied, the reproductions of the paintings, the journal articles. I once read that any biography is a siege laid by one personality against another. I don't know if this is what I'm trying to do with Poussin. I am a person who is supposed to be able to spin a clear line out of the tangle of the past, to sift the facts from the extraneous material. All I know is that I cannot think as I should be able to if I was a true resident in the world of ideas. All I know is what I cannot do.

'Nicolas Poussin,' Joseph says from the doorway, drawing out the vowels in the French way. 'How is the illustrious Monsieur Poussin?'

'Fine. Inscrutable.'

Joseph is rolling a cigarette. He runs his tongue neatly along the edge of the paper. 'Now you're in China maybe you should look at some of the Chinese artists. Find someone obscure and interesting and write a monograph.'

I surprise myself. 'Actually I've found some other research I want to do. I want to find out about the Jews who came to China during the war. There were thousands of them, you know.'

Joseph leans back in his chair. He is watching me, waiting for me to say more, but there is nothing more to be said. I don't know any more than Ken Tiger has told me. 'The wandering Jews,' he says slowly. 'They sure got around.'

'You say it like it was a choice. The wandering wasn't voluntary, it was exile.'

'It was pretty voluntary for your father. Don't think there

was much persecution to escape from in Armidale, New England.'

I stare at him across the table. He has a strange, pursed smile. I notice how much older he looks, how his clothes seem looser on him. He is peeling an apple and he lowers his eyes.

Back in Australia there was a world around us. There were friends, a house, a garden to work in on the weekends, the markets in the old boat shed where we bought our groceries. We had offices, students, good wine over dinners with colleagues. But here there are no well-worn paths around us. This is hardly a life and now we are forced back on ourselves.

I sit in silence and watch my husband eating an apple.

It's not hard to find information on the Kadoories. There are pages and pages in the library on their philanthropic works, cancer hospitals they built, local schools they founded. There are company reports, newspaper clippings, biographies. Here is Lord Kadoorie opening the Shanghai Paper Hunt Club, here are his wife and daughters feeding refugees during the war, smiling out across soup kitchens. It's like reading a fairytale.

Iraqi Jews, they came from Baghdad, made their fortunes under the protection of the British in India, moved from Bombay to Shanghai where they amassed more wealth, and then finally settled in Hong Kong after the communists took over. There's a long line of handsome sons, sent to school in England and groomed to run the family businesses.

Ada Lang is harder to find. She's not in any of the pictures; no sign of her presence in any of the stiff manila photographs of family groupings. Finally, under the Kadoorie entry in a kind of historical Who's Who of Hong Kong, I find this:

Kadoorie, Ada (nee Lang). Born Russia, 1921. Emigrated to Shanghai 1942. Married to Sir Victor Kadoorie (1903–). Arrived in Hong Kong 1946.

There's only one paragraph in Victor Kadoorie's biography about his first wife. All it says is that she was a Russian émigré who came to Shanghai during World War II and that she died shortly after the couple arrived in Hong Kong. His second wife was English and bore him five children. There's a picture of them, lined up on the curving steps of a white house. Victor is dark and handsome, the English wife pale and plump, a straw hat casting a circle of shade over her face.

Then there's a death notice, in a Hong Kong newspaper from 1947: *Kadoorie, Ada. 4 March 1947, from complications after an illness.*

Back at the apartment I pull the table up to the window and take out an empty notebook. If I lean forward I can just see the tops of the trees in the public gardens. They look like aspens. Aspens, aspens, someone once said to me, even the sound of the word lulls you into a swoon.

The sounds of the street reach me through the closed window. The endless sounds of bicycle bells and clattering engines. I open my notebook and begin to write about a death.

She exists in a kind of watery suspension. Faces float towards her and disintegrate, a woman's hands draw the shades, layers of words hover above the bed. She is liquid and indefinite, chalk-white and gaunt. Moisture gleams incandescent on her forehead.

A nurse leans towards her with a damp cloth, whispering, whispering. She is wearing a dark brooch of cut glass at her neck and Ada sees herself multiplied infinitely in its geometric refractions. Prismatic, luminous images of herself float above the bed.

This is a woman who has seen the world through the effacement of snow, who has watched, from the dark safety of winter trees, the obliteration of her own family, who has reached for a handful of snow, warm and sticky with blood. She has travelled over the vast spaces on the map, and stood on the deck of a ship speeding her to the outermost limits of the world. On the passage to China, Ada had spent hours in her cabin, her arms drawn around herself, thinking of watery deaths and feeling the sea huge and black around her suspended capsule. Despite all her inventions and re-inventions she still feels herself a trembling girl, curled in a pocket of space beneath the sea.

Somewhere is her husband, hovering at the end of the bed, talking to the doctor with his usual authoritative calm. One night she wakes suddenly to see him standing above her, staring down at her. There are deep lines between his black eyebrows. She is burning, luminous, her top lip covered in beads of moisture. From this feverish suspension she reaches out her hand to him, sees it there between them, the fingers white and bony. He looks at her for a moment longer then turns and walks from the room, closing the door behind him.

In the darkness memories rise up. This is a state of discon-nected remembering.

She remembers a boy called Vasiliy. In the summers he had told her the names of mushrooms. The bonneted baby *edulis* and the marbled *scaber*. She remembers, after an afternoon of mushroom hunting, arranging her treasures in concentric circles. She remembers the afternoon sun on the preposterous little gills and fleshy domes. She remembers Vasiliy smiling at her.

She remembers a train speeding through a black void. When she was small her mother had taken her on a trip to Moscow. They had taken the train. She remembers kneeling on a flat pillow at the breath-misted window of a sleeping car. Suddenly, out of the darkness, a handful of glowing lights that sparkled whitely and then slipped into a pocket of darkness. Later they will reappear as diamonds she wears around her neck but they will never have the same wonder as that first scattered brightness.

There are other things: the tiny footprints of a bird on new snow; a butterfly net propped against a tree; her mother sitting at a table, leaning on her elbow, her thumb pressed into her cheek close to her mouth, the pressure of it denting her skin.

She remembers her Chinese lover's arms: she remembers the way they encircled her perfectly, drawing her into a neat, warm circle. She remembers feeling his heart drum against her cheek. His heart. Its blood-pumping perfection, its containment of other, separate stories.

The nurse comes and presses a hand to her forehead. Her uniform is stiff and white. Ada turns her head to the wall. White, she remembers, the Chinese colour for death.

I don't know where these memories come from. Have they come to haunt me, the scattered recollections of a dying woman? A mad woman?

When I was small my mother took us to Sydney for a month in an old hotel above a grey beach. The hotel was run by people she knew, two elderly Russian sisters. I remember long hallways and red swirling carpets. I don't remember the look of the hotel but I can vividly recall being lifted up onto a high table in the kitchen and watching black cherries being dropped into glasses of tea. I remember lying in a cot bed under a window and peeling large flakes of paint from the wall. I can still see the exact blue of the underlayer of paint.

Sometimes my mother would disappear for long hours, leaving us with the old women. She had business in the city, she said, fastening a high button above the collarbone and shaking my clinging hands from her skirt.

My brothers would disappear into the dunes beyond the hotel and I would be left to amuse myself on the sand in front of the terrace. I wasn't allowed to go beyond the dry sand, to the place where the shore grew damp and mysterious.

Every afternoon the ladies would sit on the terrace of the hotel and talk, every afternoon of that whole summer. Friends of theirs would stop by to drink tea and talk. They would tell about their lives in Europe before the war and about the things that had happened to them and to other people. They were marvellous storytellers, and sitting on the sand under the verandah I could imagine I was in a snow-covered country estate in Russia.

After that summer I began to dream of the feel of seal furs pressed to the lips in a carriage speeding over ice. I dreamed of the warm cloud of a chestnut horse's breath on a winter morning, the thud of hooves on ice and the heavy weight of bearskin rugs. I saw cockaded footmen and pink silk-flounced skirts, onion domes of faraway cities and the purple dusks of other lands. Half-awake, I inhabited the old ladies' memories as if they were my own, as if I too had been to such a place.

But Ada Lang's memories never floated down to me from a

terrace above an Australian sea. She was a woman who died in the colony many years before I came. A mad woman.

It's not in any of the papers, but in the colony they still whisper about her madness. Raving mad, they say. A lunatic.

We had arrived in Hong Kong during the last glory days of the colony. The city was still full of people of every nation. Things would change; in time they would scatter to other cities, other postings, but then Hong Kong was swimming with the whole world. Music floated down from the windows of the Peninsula Hotel and dinners at the Indochine Restaurant lasted into the morning. Chauffeurs lined up on the sidewalk in the pale, rain-washed dawn.

Sometimes when Joseph is in the city we slip into this ceremonial life. A strange image: my husband moving among the rich, distant and faintly contemptuous.

The Peak tram line winds around the mountain like a

spidery thread. Joseph and I sit opposite each other, our knees bumping together as the carriage lumbers slowly uphill. It is dusk and the air is thick with mosquitoes.

There are people here who call the Peak Hong Kong's Mount Olympus. The higher you live on it, the higher you stand in the strange, murky welter of Hong Kong society. Once there was a time when you needed a pass to go there if you were Chinese. I suppose they didn't want the natives getting too close to the gods.

I sit quietly and watch Joseph. He looks haggard and exhausted. He stares back at me with his worn-out face, unable to smile.

'What?'

'I was thinking we should take a trip to Macau.' I'm trying for cheeriness but it comes out sounding plaintive.

'Why would we want to go to Macau?'

'Why not? It sounds interesting. All those Portuguese buildings.'

'It's all casinos and drunken businessmen. And anyway, you've barely seen anything of Hong Kong. You should go out and explore instead of sitting around reading poetry.'

'I just thought it might be nice to have a holiday together.'

'Maybe,' he says dubiously.

Sometimes I think there will always be a maze of unexplored roads between my husband and me. I've created a construct for us, the comforting shape of a marriage, and yet he still moves warily within it.

The Rays' bungalow is called Rose Cottage. It sits on a bluff halfway up the mountain. From the terrace you can look straight down at a clump of yachts moored in the harbour.

I met Clarissa Ray the week we arrived in Hong Kong. There was a Thanksgiving party at the American Embassy. I was standing alone at the bar when a woman leaned confidentially towards me. 'See that man over there propositioning that girl. He's probably suggesting dinner at the China Club. Or the honeymoon suite at the Hyatt.'

I looked over to where a heavy man with greying hair and faint patches of sweat on his shirt was standing by a girl in a sequinned dress. 'Isn't she a bit young?'

Clarissa laughed. She had a wide mouth and clear, tanned skin. She looked rich and healthy and her hair flashed brightly as the sun caught it. 'The younger the better for my husband.'

Over champagne we talked. Her husband was a wealthy American banker and she had a son at boarding school in Boston and a daughter here at the International School. Sometimes I caught faint traces of her Australian accent but it was hard to imagine her as a girl growing up in Adelaide. She told me about their last posting in Peking and the years she spent before that in India. 'My apprenticeship to the east,' she called it.

'I'm talking too much,' she said, putting her hand on my arm. It was a woman's gesture, intimate. 'My husband prefers the maid. Says at least she knows how to keep her mouth shut.'

Then she told me how she once came home from shopping to find her husband fucking the Filipina maid against the wall in the hallway. 'Just right there in the hallway, with his pants around his ankles.'

She told me this diffidently, disinterestedly, as if she were telling a story that had happened to someone else.

'What did you do?'

'Nothing. I didn't do anything.'

Perhaps I look shocked. Clarissa laughs and pats my hand. 'You silly thing. Of course in the beginning I was wild and ridiculous. I'd scream and cry and I'd smash everything up. I threw everything I could get my hands on. He'd just lie there with his eyes closed. Put a newspaper over his face.'

'He didn't say anything?'

'He said, *Don't break the Japanese vases please.*'

I don't know why Clarissa Ray singled me out to be her friend. Her confidante, as they say. She called me the week after the party at the embassy.

'Maya Wise.' Her voice was loud, liquid, trickling through the phone into my ear. In the heat of the morning I could see her in her house full of exotica, the rooms full of black wood, carved and latticed; the jade statues, the tapestries loud with silk dragons. She is a woman in a house full of objects, gazing at the shining surfaces of things.

'It's Clarissa Ray. What are you doing right now?'

She took me to lunch at the Grand Oriental Floating Restaurant. To get there you have to go down to Aberdeen fishing village and take a sampan through the maze of houseboats, fishing boats, tourist boats. Old women drive the sampans and behind their gaping grins they are quick and shrewd. The water between the boats is still and dusty, without current, although still surfaces like that can deceive you. On the decks of the houseboats scruffy looking dogs are tied up and they observe us sleepily, shaking their ears to flick away the flies as we float past. This water carries debris from the fish markets and the villages upstream: bait, fish heads, a shoe, a dead dog, a dead body.

The day Clarissa and I went there they were retrieving a body from the water. They had laid it out, covered by a stained tarpaulin between the crates of the fish market. Someone emptied out a bucket and the cloudy water trickled its way down to the covered mound, lapping at the place where the head must have been. The water was pinkish with the stain of fish entrails and to me it looked like blood, fanning out over the uneven concrete. On the other side of the market the fishermen carried on with their work, tossing thick silver fish across the barrels and shouting to each other in harsh tones.

'Poor bastard,' Clarissa said as we weaved our way through the crowd that had gathered around the body.

Over lunch she talked about her childhood, her school years in England.

'They wanted to rub off the rough provincial edges,' she laughed, 'so I could lure a good husband.'

She stared out of the window, the sun on her hair. Hanging from the ceiling was a cage of parrots, full of wild colours and almost-human calls. I wondered what tropical forests they were stolen from.

Clarissa sat and watched the parrots. 'Ruby-throated hummingbird,' she said softly. I stared at her.

'There used to be bird cards in Lipton tea boxes. My sister and I were wild for them. Luckily we drank a lot of tea in our family. There were all kinds of birds. Lots of wrens and thrushes and robins. But the rarest one was the ruby-throated hummingbird. Everyone wanted a ruby-throated hummingbird.'

She stroked her throat absent-mindedly. 'My sister got one in the end. She was just the kind of girl who would.'

There are people who, years after you have slipped free of the strange entanglements that bind lives temporarily, exist forever in a single sentence, a single moment. Long after all of this, Clarissa Ray will be a girl caught remembering a lost ruby-throated hummingbird.

After some wine Clarissa asked me about Joseph. I hesitated. I never speak about my husband. It's as if even one word could begin the release of him from my body.

'When was the first time you knew you loved him?' She is looking at me with her head tilted to one side, her palm pressed against her cheek. There's a secret pleasure in the confidences of women, a kind of confessional thrill. The blurriness of intimacy and storytelling.

Who knows when love begins?

'There was a time,' I tell her, 'in the early days, when I went to watch him play rugby. It was his one concession to his father's idea of manhood, he said. It feels like a long time ago now, standing under the eucalypts at the university oval and watching these sweating men wrestle each other with this weird kind of vigour. Joseph had this single-minded determination about it. He's the wrong build for rugby, too tall and lean. But he's strong. And stubborn.'

Clarissa's eyes are half-closed and she nods slowly, waiting for more.

'Standing there, watching the look on his face as he was fighting someone for the ball, I kept thinking that it was the same look he has when we're making love. You know, the eyes closed, the exertion. As if rapture and agony look the same.'

The boat dips and sways lightly beneath us. I don't know why I'm telling her this.

'Watching him sweating and fighting, my heart was in my mouth the whole time. I couldn't bear the thought of blows to his skin. I felt this strange, overwhelming tenderness for him. Is tenderness the same as love?'

After lunch Clarissa took me to a pearl shop. There were hundred of strands of pearls lined up like bobbly seaweed under the glass. Ivory pearls, pink pearls, pearls as smooth and round as marbles, and odd, lumpy-shaped pearls. A bowing salesman fastened a strand of black pearls around my neck and held a mirror up for me. They shone darkly in the hollows of my collarbone. While Clarissa bought pearl earrings and pearl bracelets, I lifted a strand to my lips, rubbing them against my teeth to see if they were real. They felt gritty and salty, like sand.

The Rays' reception rooms are vast, like some elegant hotel. There are elaborate arrangements of orchids in each corner. Outside, the sky has turned dark red and raindrops are splattering on the terrace. Somewhere a dog is barking.

Most of the women are wearing pale colours. They're best for the summers. The cool fall of fine linen, the soft lines of silk. They look young and fresh, like schoolgirls at a dance. People are talking about the Handover. Right around the corner now, someone is saying.

'Are people worried?' I ask one of the men.

'There's nothing for us to worry about. It's in their

interests to let us be. They're a clever lot, the Chinese. Making money is all they really care about. Hong Kong wouldn't be what it is without the foreign interest.'

Joseph smiles. There's a kind of cruelty in his smile sometimes. 'I think Maya might have been referring to the six million Hong Kong Chinese,' he says, 'rather than our cosy bunch of ex-pats.'

The room is silent. I look down at my hands. They look like my mother's, worn and thin. Someone laughs uncomfortably. Geoffrey Ray claps a heavy hand around Joseph's shoulders. 'I've lived with the Chinese for twenty years. You don't have to worry about that lot. They always get by.'

'I'm sure they do.'

'And we hear you're something of a historian too,' someone says to me. 'Art history, isn't it? Who's your favourite artist?'

Joseph puts his arm lightly around me. 'My wife,' he says, 'refuses to be seduced by modern art. She's very unfashionable really. Her great heroes are Poussin and Rembrandt. You really must get hold of her if you want a comprehensive lecture on seventeenth century Dutch portraiture.'

I think of a time, years ago, when I lay in Joseph's arms watching the sun play over his face.

'Tell me,' he said, 'why you love Rembrandt so much.'

I leaned on my elbow, my face above his. 'His portraits,' I told him, 'are not so much posed as *caught*. As if he had snuck up and surprised the sitter. The identity is there in the imperfections. The slightly open mouth, the startled expression, the ink-stained fingers. I like the idea that character might be most candidly exposed when caught unaware. Rembrandt anticipated photography. Not in the sense of the duplication of a face, but in the way he could capture the entirety of a character in the revelation of a single instant. A life from which a single moment has been shorn away.'

'My wife,' he said, 'the eternal teacher.'

I looked down at his own face, so composed, the lines carefully arranged in the depiction of a mildly amused smile.

It's the same face he has now, years later, leaning against a window in the Hong Kong dusk.

Later, at the dinner table, they bow their heads to pray. *Bless us O Lord and these thy gifts*. Eyes closed, hands together, they look earnest, harmless. Joseph and I glance at each other across the table. *Shabbat Shalom*, I mouth to him. He frowns and looks away.

Shabbat Shalom. Joseph had a Jewish grandfather and for years he had clung to that strand of imagined Jewishness. He wanted desperately to be Jewish, he told me once. In the long, drowsy hours after lovemaking we would lie under the blankets, our bodies pressed to each other, and tell stories. The stories always had the tone of secrets, the bed the shadowy dimness of the confessional.

He was, he said, obsessed with the idea of a cultural condition of wandering, of suffering always there, like a mathematical constant. He thought that Jewishness would somehow provide a framework for his own suffering, for his family's suffering. It was as if pain, he whispered, was something that ran in the blood.

He adored the aesthetics: the Hebrew language and its throat-catching thickness, the dark spareness of the synagogues and the sonorous hum of the prayers. He loved the heavy dark eyes of the women, the Jewish eyes, and he loved the grand narratives of suffering, of dislocation and loss. He still remembers the words. *Driven away from their burning city, the Jews shall live in graves for the next twenty centuries.*

He had a Jewish friend at university and would go home with him for Shabbat meals. This custom he remembers most: at the end of the meal the father would make sure that all the knives were removed from the table. When Joseph asked them the reason they told him that in reciting the customary blessing in which Jerusalem, the holy city, the lost homeland, was mentioned, there was the risk that the grief-stricken Jew would take the knife and plunge it into his heart. It was best that this temptation be removed.

I remember Jerusalem, the dislocation of Jerusalem. In the dusty heat of the Australian four o'clock I am a girl sitting cross-legged on a dry log, a heavy book on her knees. It is an old book, torn, with yellowing pages. In that book is Jerusalem. There are pictures of high walls and curved domes, earnest pilgrims and a great orange orb settling over the rooftops. There are narrow streets and beggars with burning eyes. Everywhere, there are people praying. In the red dirt of the Australian outback, Jerusalem was a city that existed safely in books, and in books it was to be found.

It is a dual memory, the Jerusalem memory, and it stands striking, lucid. No dream-caught fragment. In the yard, above the pages of the Jerusalem book, my brothers have dragged a kangaroo they've found hit by a truck. There is its face, its dull dead fur, its glass eyes. They're preparing for a skinning and I can see the flash of their pocket knives. My brothers, their mud-caked boots and their soiled canvas shirts, the stale, sweet smell of them.

I watch them drag the animal across the bald grass by its tail, its pretty face rubbing in the dirt. I watch the legs splay apart, the knife pierce with strange deftness the pale fluff of the belly and zigzag downwards through the length of the carcass. The blade swishes neatly under the skin and fur is ripped away from flesh. I watch over the rooftops of Jerusalem as the chest is exposed in all its veiny, glistening pinkness. Beneath the dusty fur and the pale green layer of fat there is a universe of colour. Deep reds and dark traceries of blue, patches of yellow and stretched pink sinews. I stare transfixed.

Above the red sky of Jerusalem are the heads of my brothers, bent intently over their work, the arcs of their knives working the pelt away from the once-living animal. They roll the skin, kangaroo-shaped, into a scroll and wipe their knives clean on their trouser legs.

Sometimes I wonder if Joseph, when he saw me with my dark eyes and Jewish name, fell in love with an image, a shade.

I want to write about Ada Lang. In the Kadoorie narrative she is a shadow, or merely the memory of a shadow. A false step in some other, more known, more important story.

I find traces of story everywhere. At the Hong Kong Club people still remember her. Hardly any of them are old enough to have known her, but stories about her abound: she was so beautiful men turned in the streets, so wicked she frequented opium dens and slept with Chinese men, so mad she lost her mind. She is a fallen woman, a temptress, a martyr, a saint. She drifts, this woman, unknowable, veiled by her mythical hair.

I am going to look for Ada Lang. I will pick her up at that moment when her ship comes sailing into Shanghai

Harbour. When she first began to stir, to move toward me.

Shanghai. Who knows the beginnings of a city? Shanghai, rising like a dream from the wide, lazy loop of the Whangpoo River. A fisherman leaning on a spear, resin torches, fish nets and the mists of the shallows. A village built on shifting mudflats, as unstable as memory. A city at once reaching skywards and sinking.

The years fold up neatly. Spread them out like the pleated arc of a Chinese fan. Here are the merchants, the whole world pouring through their fingers: spices, tea, gold dust, crepe de Chine, Shandong silk, chests of opium. Then the Englishmen, the French, the buckles and brass, the twirling moustaches, the sleek lines of the clippers, the strange, sweet smell of opium. The buildings, flaring up like cathedrals along the Bund, the powdered wives stepping tentatively from wave-lapped cocoons of floating space into the clamour of China.

Then the missionaries, their white veils billowing like sails, their eyes raised to God as they pick their way through the stench of the alleys. And the White Russians, from St Petersburg, from Siberia, running from a red peril. On Easter, crowds of them carrying tall white tapers and crying 'Christos voskresi.' On the street they call Blood Alley, shop signs in Cyrillic script swing above their heads. At the Venus Cafe you can pay ten cents to dance with a Russian countess.

And last of all, the Jews. Not the rich Iraqi Jews with their marble palaces, but the Jews of Europe. The Jews of Russia, of Germany, of Poland. In the shored-up trap of Europe, Shanghai presents itself as a destination. *Shanghai*, they murmur to themselves, needing only to say the word to conjure up thoughts of freedom, of escape, of a China-blue world miles away from the tongues of the flame. Shanghai, the only port in the world not requiring a visa or entry papers.

They come across the blank space of Siberia, that strange-looking glass world, the distances that are too great. They come across the Sea of Japan, on ships down the lazy yellow river. Shanghai flows past them in old Chinese streets, wet and heavy with the stench of flesh, of songbirds in wicker cages and baskets of flapping fish.

They are herded in trucks to damp barracks, where sheets are strung to divide families, to muffle the sounds of grief, the sounds of love. They boil water to drink, they bend over their prayer books, they line up for cups of rice.

Dressed in heavy European clothes they tramp from door to door in the French Concession selling coffee cups, old silver, Bohemian glass, fur coats. Along the Bund they spread out their books with water-stained pages.

This is Shanghai.

Ada Lang stands on the deck as China flares into existence. She is heavy-eyed, narrow-shouldered, her hair a fiery thicket. It is summer and already the air is cloying. She cups her hands around her eyes to make a tunnel of shade.

The harbour is crowded with boats: gunships with wavering flags, opium clippers, merchant boats and fishing junks, and sampans poled by old women. The water is the colour of slick oil. On the dock, bare-chested coolies run up and down planks, old ladies with bound feet stagger past children and beggars, incense and spirit-money peddlers shout their wares, and rickshaws line up along the road. Beyond them a Sikh policeman in a red turban blows on his whistle.

From one of the ships men are unloading an enormous golden tabernacle, lowering it into a waiting sampan with an elaborate system of ropes. They call out to each other and strange syllables float over the water. Two nuns watch anxiously from the dock.

Ada Lang watches her reflection in the tabernacle. In the gold-gleam she can see all the distortions of her face, its features expanded, lengthened, multiplied. This is no mirror, with its faithfully rendered reflection, this is light-spiked, multifaceted refraction. A face in all its possibilities.

In our room above the street Joseph shows me pictures of mummies found in the desert. There is one they call the Beauty of Loulan. She is as old as Abraham, Joseph tells me, holding the picture up to the light.

The Beauty of Loulan's skin is blackened with age but her features have been perfectly preserved by the desert sands. She has fine lips and a high slender nose. Her face is decorated with coloured whorls like tattoos. She has long red hair and a robe of indigo wool with a feather sticking up from her hood. In the photograph it looks as if she is smiling.

'Do you know what Iksander said when we found her?' Joseph asks. Iksander is one of his Uighur guides. I have never seen him. 'He said *this is the most beautiful woman in the world. If she was alive today I would make her my wife.* The most beautiful woman in the world.'

On the map of China the far northern regions are coloured in various shades of brown. Landlocked, no blue line of a river marks these parts, no lake or inland sea. Only tiny circles of khaki scattered on the edges of the desert. These are the oasis towns. There is a vast sand sea and a mountain range whose name translates as 'The Roof of the World'.

In one of Joseph's books is a map that shows the former kingdoms of the desert, the vanished northern cities and the lines of trade routes that once crisscrossed the Sand Sea. The darkest line is Marco Polo's Silk Road. Circles of colour symbolise the produce and the riches of each region, the goods that were exchanged for gold.

Joseph tells me about the scraps of life he finds in the desert. A perfectly preserved clay spoon. A felt hat. A baby's bottle made of stretched goat skin. In the desert you are always surrounded by lost history. And then this prehistoric woman, buried beneath the shifting dunes.

Today the Beauty of Loulan lies in a laboratory in England. She had to be saved from the Chinese. In her home in the north there are ardent Muslims who gouge the eyes out of statues and destroy sculptures, people to whom the word science is an empty sound. And in the centres of power are men with other reasons to destroy her. With her aquiline features, her red hair and her high, slender nose, she bears little racial affinity to the Han Chinese who claim they are the most ancient inhabitants of the northern deserts.

So she was carted away to cold countries and teams of forensic archaeologists. They took scrapings from her bones and catalogued her clothing. Every month there were new discoveries. Her age, her weight, a reconstruction of her face in life, complete with the cascading red hair that had made her famous. Joseph greeted every new revelation as if he were learning the intricacies of a lover. One day they will all be in the book he will write about her, a book that will change forever the history of the desert and the people who lay claim to it.

It is not these stories that interest me. There is another, smaller story.

In the sand next to the Beauty of Loulan's desert grave archaeologists found the tiny corpse of a baby. A child less than a year old with perfectly preserved curls of hair and blue stones pressed over her eyes. Carefully folded into the grave was a felt bonnet, a tiny fur cloak and a small cup. Tests showed that the baby was no blood relation to the Beauty of Loulan. The little girl was not her baby. The scientists can think of no explanation for the presence of this child.

I need a better story. I want to know how the Beauty of Loulan came to die in the desert with another woman's child by her side. Was her tribe stricken by illness or war? Did a dead mother bequeath this obviously well-loved child to her? Did she try to keep the baby alive with goats' milk?

I ask Joseph these questions and he says that archaeologists are scientists, not novelists. They can reconstruct the facts but not the stories of the past.

'Not everything fits, Maya,' he says, packing away the photographs spread across the table. 'Not everything has a neat story.'

Tomorrow he is going away. His work takes him back to the desert, up into China and out of my reach. Already he is distracted, distant, one eye on the desert. I lay my hand on the back of his neck. The skin is warm and smooth.

'Want to go for a gin and tonic? It's too hot in here,' I say.

'I've got to sort out my notes. I'll have one with you when I get back.'

I say nothing and he looks faintly impatient. 'Cheer up. It's only a couple of weeks.'

I take my hand away from his neck.

Once I asked him to take me to the desert. It is not completely unheard of for a wife to come along on the shorter trips. To sit with a wide-brimmed hat in the shade of the tents, to sketch the sand dunes and pour the men rum mixed with lime juice at the end of the day's work.

I will always remember what he said to me. 'Why do women want everything of a man?'

It's always been there in my husband, this old desire for self-sufficiency, the need to slide away and apart. It used to make me angry, the walls he put up around himself, his idea that he could live in a world apart from the mess and mire of human affections, that he didn't need the words *in love*. He thought this was a virtue.

Once he said to me, 'The best way is to expect nothing of people. That way you can never be disappointed.' We were lying in bed when he said it and I turned away and slipped out from under his arm. I stood in the doorway and looked down at him in the bed. 'I think you are inhuman,' I said.

He smiled. 'Well, I'll just be inhuman then and have my peace.'

His peace. I didn't speak to him for three days.

Darkness between us as we sit across the table from each other. We need a garden to walk in, a moon over the water and swerving candlelight. Joseph's head is bent over his papers, his lips making shapes around Chinese words as if he wants to slip away into his own spell, as if murmuring an incantation.

'Do you remember the races?'

He looks up. 'Fighting Fox.'

'And you in your father's hat.'

Once we had gone to the races to bet on horses. It was summer, one of the first hot days, and flies clung to the backs of men's shirts. Neither of us had ever been before. We didn't know anything about horses or about betting. We sat on a bench beside the track and studied the form guide. We read about the horses' spirits and their temperaments, their recent wins and failures. The form guide read like someone was talking to you, like an old racing bloke was having a yarn. 'Not the roughest,' it said if the horse was a fairly good prospect.

Joseph and I liked the sound of a horse called Fighting Fox. The guide said he was brave and proud, that he only ran when he wanted to. We went and had a look at him. He glared angrily under his forelock and stamped his hoof cleverly on the jockey's foot. Joseph went down to the bookies' circle and put fifty dollars on him. It seemed like an enormous amount of money.

'Remember how excited the crowd was?' I say. 'How we laughed at them calling out to the horses, as if they could hear them, but then we were doing it too. We did it properly, grabbing onto each other and yelling at Fighting Fox to go faster.'

'Fighting Fox. He was a good old runner.'

'You were so excited. You grabbed my hand so hard and you had your other hand on your heart. I'd never seen you so concentrated on anything before. And then you kissed me when he won.'

'It was your birthday, wasn't it? And we went to that restaurant in Northbridge. The Moon. And spent all our money on ridiculous cocktails.'

'We walked home drunk and you sang in French. We were so happy.'

Joseph stares at me across the table. 'It's strange for you here, isn't it?'

'Yes.'

He nods and his body makes a movement of shadow. 'Aurel Stein thinks there are more mummies out there. Where we found the Beauty of Loulan. Older, maybe.'

'Maybe they don't want to be dug up.' I sound petulant, even to myself. The clinging lover. *Trailing wives*, they call them here.

Joseph sighs. 'Do you know how close Stein and I are to proving that the Chinese didn't get to the Tarim Basin first? What that might mean for the Uighur tribes, for their independence?'

'I didn't know you were so interested in politics.'

'It's not just politics. It's a human rights issue. Haven't you been reading the papers? All the disappearances, the torture, the brutality?'

'Oh. I must have missed that.'

'Missed it? How do you live here and miss something like that?'

'Chinese politics isn't my interest, it's yours.' Even to myself I sound petulant and childish.

'You *used* to find politics interesting,' Joseph says archly. I say nothing.

He stops and puts his hands on my shoulders as he walks to the bedroom. 'You'll find yourself something to do.'

I can feel the warmth of his flesh through the thin cotton of my dress. This time tomorrow he will be away in the desert.

When Joseph is away, it is not sex but simply touch that I crave the most. A pair of hands on my shoulders, the smooth length of his spine on the nights we sleep back to back, skin pressed together from shoulder to hip. The pressure of his ribcage against mine when he collapses on top of me, his hot breath against my neck.

When I met Joseph he was already famous among the strange international cult of archaeologists. He was the man who spoke the languages of China flawlessly, who had trekked across more than half of the Taklamakan Desert, the protégé of the famous sinologist Aurel Stein. He had published a brilliant monograph on the history of the lost tribes of the Tarim Basin, another on Lop Nor, had already made a name for himself as an eloquent and assiduous scholar.

But at the university where we both taught all this was half-buried. The Faculty of Arts was in thrall to a particular kind of French critical theory and there was little interest in the arcane world of the men who dug up the desert. Ours was an age of postmodernists. We averted our eyes from fields that clung too closely to the rigours of science. We were not interested in catalogued facts.

Joseph had occupied the office down the hall from me for over two years and I had only a vague idea of what it was he did. He was a tall man in pale shirts with hair that curled beautifully away from his temples. He was scrupulously polite and formal, distracted-looking at faculty meetings, strict with his students. A man who gave the impression of impatience barely contained. He sat alone in the dining room at University House, buried in a book or a newspaper or staring out at the birds swooping above the river.

Mornings by the river. I see him there, swathed in light. In the dining hall the light is from the river and the pale sky beyond. He leans forward to pour more tea and the light falls on his neck, his face. His legs are long and crossed gracefully. He brings his hands together, each fingertip touching.

Once, standing in front of a poster advertising a James Joyce conference on the faculty noticeboard, I turned to see him beside me, holding his leather satchel.

'When I read *Ulysses* I rewarded myself at the end of each chapter by composing a limerick summarising the chapter.'

I look at him, at his high, clever forehead and half-smile.

'How wonderful. You could publish them. A kind of study-guide. Or a substitute for lazy students.'

'Yes, but I might need to find an Irish publisher. I can't imagine there'd be much of a market for it here.'

'No.'

He was not popular in university circles. He was too stern and single-minded, so absorbed in his work that he made those around him feel somehow inadequate. He always worked late; there were many nights when his light was on long after midnight. He had an aloof, distant manner with his colleagues. He only occasionally slipped in and out of university functions, always giving the impression that he found the social world around him irrelevant.

I had peered through the open door of a lecture room once and seen him bent over a book with some students, telling them almost joyfully about the face of a mummy found in the desert. He leaned back in his chair, drawing the shape of the body with his hands, his face flushed with sudden excitement. I had never seen him so animated.

That summer, inexplicably, he sent me a postcard from one of his field trips to the desert. A picture of a seascape.

In the desert there are odd echoes of other worlds.
Sometimes a fossilised seashell, or the skeleton of a fish.

Sometimes a dune that looks like a wave. It is not surprising to find that a great prehistoric sea once filled this place.

And then his name, scrawled above a line of Chinese stamps.

In my office by the river, I imagine him in a circle around a campfire, drinking tea with the Uighur guides he has written about, the ones who can find water by the slight discoloration at the foot of a dune.

In his book he had written that at twilight in the desert there is no sound but the hiss of sand being blown off the ridges. It's a kind of singing, he wrote.

He was the anomaly in our midst, the true explorer in a world of words and talk. A finder and namer of things, leaning forward to pour a cup of tea, the light on his face and neck as he stirred his sugar.

It never occurred to me that light can deceive you, that in the desert things lose their shape and float towards you in trembling distortion.

I am reading Pliny. In the chapter on the history of sculpture he tells a story about the Corinthian maid, Diboutade. On learning that her lover was to go away to war she had him sit by a wall with the sun behind him. Taking a stick of charcoal she carefully traced the outline of his profile on the wall. Later her father, the potter Boutades, filled in the charcoal lines with damp clay, creating a kind of portrait relief.

I prefer the daughter's shadowy souvenir. I want the wavering memory. The nebulous memento. Without the edges firmed up.

'In the beginning,' says Ken Tiger, 'the Jews came very

slowly. A few men, perhaps a young couple. There was a place for them. There were other Jews, you have to remember. Wealthy ones from Iraq and then from Russia. The ones that came before the war. They had their own world, we never saw much of them. They were just more foreigners to us. But then they started to come by the hundreds. There would be trucks to meet them at the dock. I remember watching them come off the ships. They looked poor. And afraid. I felt sorry for them.'

I can see them, these people. Their lives have fallen into two pieces, divided by more than an ocean.

In the beginning, before there were so many, the Shanghai Jews found rooms for them, jobs in their businesses, money to set up their own shops. In the beginning there was a place for them but then, as Europe burned, there were too many for the small community to absorb. By the middle of the war there were more than ten thousand. They set up relief committees, passed around hats, sent telegrams to America for help. But the eyes of the world were elsewhere.

This is the beginning of Ada Lang's story. This is the history of a small pocket of Jews in China.

The bewildered Jewish refugees were hastily packed into abandoned houses, military barracks and empty warehouses. The dwelling Ada is allocated is in an old house on Chusan Road which has been divided with thin sheets of plywood into tiny apartments. She shares a dim room on the second floor with a family of German Jews, the Hakhams. At night she sleeps with the daughter of the family, Hadassah.

Lying in bed in the early mornings Ada watches the heat form in breath-like clouds on the window pane. Already the thin sheet is sodden, her hair damp and heavy. Shanghai is drowning in the summer monsoon.

Outside, on the street, the noise is cataclysmic. This is the

Chinese city. Horses' hooves striking the pavement like anvils and the screeching clang of trolley cars. Hawkers shouting, blind men sounding brass gongs, birds squawking in wicker baskets and throngs of people. The noise of the street fills the apartment. It drifts in damp clouds of air laden with dust and pollen.

Chaim Hakham sits by the window, silent, still and heavy as the statues of Buddha Ada has seen through the gates of temples and on small shrines behind shop counters. Once a year, on the birthday of Lord Buddha, the Chinese take their statues from monasteries and temples and ceremoniously bathe them in water scented with sandalwood, ambergris, turmeric and aloes. Afterwards the water is drunk by the faithful.

The Jews have their own rituals but there is no space for them here. This is not like the dark ghettoes of Europe but they are painfully poor. Twice a day they take a tin pot and line up by a window where food is distributed by the relief committee. They get one ladle in the pot for each member of the household. Back in their room Naima Hakham stirs in semolina, which can be bought on the black market.

Naima has things that can be sold for food. One by one she draws her treasures out of the tin trunk. The silver tea service is not in the usual style. The pieces are heavy and slightly irregular with handles that form dramatic curlicues. Ada imagines a long-ago silversmith, tired of small contained gestures, fixing in place a spout that flourishes like an elephant's trunk. There is a gold bracelet inlaid with stone scarab beetles. The enamelled blueness of the beetles is far more dazzling than the dull gleam of the surrounding gold. It seems an odd thing for a German woman to have. There are crystal earrings shaped like small flowers and a necklace made of beads of jet. There are other things that won't bring any money. Ada runs her fingers across a heavily embroidered cloth, the stitches so small and dense they look like tapestry. The underside of the cloth is filled with small knots where the embroiderer has changed thread. Naima sells swathes of handmade lace to a Chinese grocer for fresh vegetables. With potatoes she makes a kind of goulash. Some onions, some paprika and instead of meat, boiled potatoes. In the evenings they sit around one sputtering candle and Naima tells stories about other candle lit evenings in warm houses by a dark forest. It's not Ada's language but the voice, low and soft, is soothing.

Some of the refugees have gathered enough money to lease an empty hall for a synagogue. They string sheets across the centre of the room to separate the men and women. There are plenty of planks and crates for benches and someone has brought their leather-bound Torah. The leather is patchy and stained where it has been ruined by seawater. On Shabbat the air is thick with sounds of Hebrew and the quiet murmur of prayers. In the synagogue the world is firm and orderly. The Torah is divided into fifty-four exactly composed sections, one to be read each week until the cycle is completed. It is possible to live within a system of elegant and discrete weekly universes.

Ada sits among the women and remembers the dark wood and stained glass of the synagogues of Russia. She thinks of the line of bent heads that had been the women of her family. Once she had looked over to see her mother's face lit up with the refractions of light through the coloured glass of the window. Her whole face was speckled with hovering diamonds of green and blue. She had seemed so complete, so enclosed in her own contemplations, so oblivious to her daughter's errant thoughts. Head bent over her prayer book, she had the composure and self-containment of a prophet, the rapture of a mystic. She had never seemed so separate.

Years later, in a small room rank with the sweet smells of brass and sweat, Ada wonders if she might ever exist in the same self-enclosed universe. Beside her Hadassah drags her feet back and forth on the floor and pushes her sharp elbow into Ada's ribs.

At night, pressed between the wall and Hadassah's thin back she hears the muffled sounds of weeping and the heavy scurrying sounds of a rat. From another part of the house comes a high keening wail. Ada thinks of the house as a giant heart, all intimate cavities and secret chambers, all straining inwards and pulsating with shared grief.

Her own heart, disembodied and riddled with loss,

contracts painfully, closing in on itself. She wakes gasping for breath, her chest tight, her body unclaimed, nationless.

Shanghai, Ada Lang whispers to herself, the very sound of the word mysterious, undecipherable. She stands, framed by a low doorway, the city a gaping labyrinth before her.

It is the very unknowableness of the place that frightens and fascinates her. She is a girl used to seeing the world through a nimbus of snow. Here is a city of a thousand watery alleys and false turns, a city built on ground so porous that one engineer described it as not much more solid than dirty water. From her doorway she sees countless lighted windows gleaming like the eyes of devils, wisps of smoke rising from a hundred coal stoves. Faces, irretrievably foreign, leer at her from the yellow circles of paraffin lamps.

In the first days Shanghai was unreal, a city where everything happened as if it were not so, as if it were a dream. Walking home from the kitchens, holding a cloth over a pot of thin soup, a Chinese girl came towards her, a baby in her arms. She was begging and she held the baby out to Ada, whining in a low voice. The baby seemed fast asleep, its eyes closed heavily, its head lolling to one side. Ada reached out to touch its face. The skin was stiff and cold. The child was dead. Ada cried out and drew her hand back and the girl began to laugh. She sat down on the side of the road, rocking the filthy bundle in her arms and laughing a strange high laugh. Ada clutched the soup pot and ran, her boots making sparks against the flagstones.

Another day she pressed herself against a wall as a dark column of men surged past her. Dressed in the heavy clothes of Europe, prayer books in their hands, they moved as one body. The narrow street was black with them. The whole of the Mir Yeshiva School had made it to Shanghai. Three hundred of them, rabbis, teachers and students, had fled Poland through Vilna and Lithuania on Japanese transit visas. *A Chinese miracle*, people whispered to each other. Somehow they had raised the funds to build a makeshift synagogue and every day they could be seen walking hurriedly to worship. Ada watched them as they passed. Some of them were only boys. Pale teenagers with their sidelocks and newly sprouting beards. They looked devout and purposeful, a self-contained throng, radiating invisible holy light. Sometimes they nodded sternly at her and she thought that perhaps she should be able to communicate with them, her own pale-faced people. But to her they seemed too strange and substantial in a world whose edges were constantly dissolving and remaking themselves.

Ada begins to go walking. Every day she walks further from the house on Chusan Road. She finds herself in a maze-world of alleys and dark courtyards, the covered paths that are the heart of the Chinese city. Everything is mysterious. She stops to stare at a row of jars containing curled snakes suspended in brown liquid. Cages full of frogs sit next to stacks of live crabs wrapped in ribbons of banana leaves. Market stalls offer wild arrays of fruits more colourful and stranger than any she has ever seen. All around her crowds move and push, people slide past her carrying baskets of produce, balancing poles across their shoulders. There is a dank smell of fish and incense, smoke and tiger balm. On the side of the street men sit at small food stalls, eating noodles with chopsticks, their bowls raised close to their mouths. They stare at her as she passes. Their eyes, Ada thinks, are too dark to hold your gaze. If you look into them they give you back nothing but your own image.

In Hong Kong it's nearly Christmas and the streets have been festooned with tinsel and gaudy Santa Clauses. The first time I saw the decorations hanging above the traffic I caught my breath in surprise. Could it possibly be Christmas here?

Joseph teases me for loving this season. He finds it crass, commercialised, even depressing. But it's so expectant, so full of hope.

Christmas in the colonies. I wonder if it was the same everywhere, in the other colonies, as it is here in Hong Kong. I can see them in my imagination, the others like us, like the men at the Hong Kong Club. The Christmas drinks, the wives decorating the villas and teaching the servants how to make plum pudding. The Christmas lunches at the big hotels.

We are going to the Christmas party at the Hong Kong Club. An obligation, says Joseph, pulling at his tie, frowning at himself in the mirror. Looking at his reflection I think that he has aged, the hair thinning slightly from his high forehead, creases around his eyes from too many days of squinting into desert light.

Watching him, I think of the early days, when desire first began. I remember the first time he reached out his hand and placed it on my bare knee. We were both silent, staring at each other. *Maya*, he said finally, as if it were an admission of something.

I remember the first time I saw him undressed, his eyes as we both looked down. The feel of him, throbbing almost in time with the heart, the darkness of the blood beneath the fine skin. He took my hand and raised it to his lips and ran his tongue along the palm. I love your hands, he said, as if love began with outer limbs.

In the beginning there was *making love,* but never shared sleep. It was a space he kept for himself. He never wanted a body just for warmth, for the comfort of sleep. He slept easily, turning his face away from the world and curling into self-contained sleep. I wanted to lie against his body all night, to be like other lovers with their laziness of sleep, their slow mornings. Even to sleep beside him like a sister.

But he would not allow it. He needed to sleep alone, he said. Needed a clear mind for the day ahead.

Sometimes he would fall asleep while I was still dressing to leave. I would stand at the end of the bed, slipping my feet into shoes, irritated by his self-sufficiency, by my own need.

Later I realised that it was one of his ways of protecting himself. He knew the trick of keeping people on the periphery. Sometimes when he rose above me in bed, his chest damp, his arms taut, I would feel invisible to him, to his lost, distant look. It was only when he cried out and fell against my breasts that he returned to me. *Stay*, I would say to him, wanting his weight. Wanting his heavy, moving chest against me.

It was only after the first winter that he called me to him in the night. I had been working on a paper for a conference all week. Staying in my office until the early hours drinking cup after cup of good coffee and eating chocolate. 'Like a happy pig,' I laughed to him over the phone. And it's true, I did love those long nights of fierce concentration, the pools of light and the empty corridors.

I was peeling back the skin of milk from a hot cup of coffee when he called. He sounded faraway and exhausted. He said he was sick. Dizziness and a fever. He hadn't been out of bed for two days. Could I come?

I walked towards his house by the river. The night was

calm and damp, the air full of the warm, weedy smells of the river. There was only the faint swish of the trees and the moonlight bouncing off the leaves of the peppermints along the river. From the street I could see the glow of the verandah light. A welcoming light, a light he had switched on for me.

I walked through the garden, towards Joseph's light and the door he had left open. The apartment was dark but I knew every turn and doorway, the number of steps from the hall to his bed. I put my ear against his sleeping chest, the skin hot and dry, the heart beating steadily. He moved and reached his arms out as I crawled in against his body. I lay against him, feeling his heat through my own skin, watching the drifting landscape of clouds through the window. He kissed the top of my head, his lips against my hair. Outside, the peppermint trees made a sieve for the moonlight. We slept that night under silver shadows.

In Hong Kong it's a typhoon day. One of those afternoons when the clouds are a dense black bank and the whole city seems battened down waiting for the onslaught. Up on the Peak a thick, reeking curtain of fog has settled over the summit and clouds of moisture prickle warningly all over the city.

Inside the club the air is cold and clammy. There are so many people to kiss, the men thrusting their faces close and leaving warm patches of moisture on my cheeks. *Merry*

Christmas. Or should we say, Happy Hanukkah! Smug laughter, because they know what it is. I don't need to say much. The women are more restrained. They sip martinis and proffer cool dry cheeks, pointing out which of the squabbling children belong to them.

I can recognise the British women. Pale and slightly blowsy, they cluster together as if they were in the member's enclosure at Ascot. I wonder if it will be over soon, all of this. Royal Hong Kong, the prized colony, the Union Jack rising reassuringly against the hazy Chinese skyline, all these people gathered together under the British flag. Whatever it had been, it was ending.

The Arts and Crafts Society made the decorations, one of the women tells me; they had been working for weeks, especially on the wreaths. The wreaths had been the big project this year. We admire the huge wreath above the stage, festooned with pine cones and tinsel. Beneath it a Chinese Santa Claus is sitting on one of the big oak chairs from the Jackson Room, a pair of blonde children on his knee. I should join the society really, she says, they might do a quilt in the new year, although it was hard with so many people always leaving and coming.

The women talk about the long vacations to Europe and the trips home where they pass their photographs around and talk about the strange life of the colonies. They talk about the heat and the sun and the children, about the husbands. They tell me, all of them, what companies their husbands work for. In Hong Kong a name is not enough, it has to be tied to something, defined by something. There is nothing for me to add after my name. They sip their shandies and bat Chinese fans at their chins.

Aurel Stein is there, Joseph's beloved Stein. He has a small dog in his arms.

'And how is the beautiful wife?' he says to me. In some ways he is like Joseph. He is a man who will never unknot himself. I run my hand through the silky hair of his dog. It feels like the hair of a small child. The dog is called Dash. Stein has had a succession of these fox terriers, seven in total, all named Dash. Days after one dies in its sleep or misjudges its step on a cliff in the desert, another Dash appears, as if loss can always be replaced.

The seeds of Joseph's obsession with China lie far back in another story. The person who planted them is Aurel Stein. If I want to understand Joseph, then I have to start with Stein.

Aurel Stein was the first westerner to begin excavating the Chinese deserts. He had been a famous archaeologist in Germany, his early career interrupted by the war and four years spent hiding in a cattle barn on a farm in the south. He used those years to study the languages of China.

In the fifties he made a name for himself as a sinologist. He buried himself in the ancient world, researching exhaustively and writing elegantly about the context of Asian cultures. He travelled to the remotest parts of China, leading teams of archaeologists and anthropologists, presiding over digs in the desert and passing round rum and lime juice by the fire at night. In Europe, China was a dim curiosity, a place faintly exotic and faraway, but to Stein it was the centre of the world. He walked through the streets of Berlin, his eye always on some other landscape.

For as long as I've known him he's had a great curve of silver hair and a handkerchief poking neatly out of his chest pocket. When I met him for the first time he raised his hands in a gesture of mock surprise. 'Ah! The beautiful writer at last!' Over dinner I could feel him watching me, his eyes travelling dispassionately over my face, over the globes of amber glinting at my ears, the long hair. He had a thin, firm mouth.

After we had eaten, he and Joseph disappeared into the study, the excited rise and fall of their voices echoing in the hallway. Soon they were speaking Chinese. They were planning an expedition, tracing out lines on a map, writing lists.

I walked slowly around the lounge room, staring at the dark landscape paintings on the walls. Aurel Stein had poured me a glass of sherry. 'German sherry,' he said, 'the best in the world.'

Joseph had met Stein in his second year at the university by the river. In all the years of his childhood, Joseph had rarely come to the city. There had been the house at the far edge of the eastern suburbs, the ragged paddocks and market gardens beyond, the tiny town centre and the local high school where most of the boys left at fifteen to follow their fathers into trades.

On hot summer nights he would steal down the hallway, past the room where his father slept, and sit on the front steps staring out at the sickle-shaped moon and the empty street. Huge moths flapped under the porch light. Early on he had found the piles of his mother's books stacked neatly in the woodshed and he read them at the kitchen table in the evenings after his father had gone to bed. He was more interested in the exotic places described than the stories themselves, which he found unrealistic and boring. He looked up the place names in the dusty atlas in the school library. None of them was ever in Australia. His mother he remembered only as a vague outline, prone on her bed with endless migraines, sitting at the table by the window for hours on end with a cup of cooling tea clasped in her hands.

At school Joseph was clever and fast, surprising his teachers with the essays he produced in History and English classes. They read sections out to the class and pinned them up in the staffroom next to the tea roster. The reports that were sent home to his father were full of rows of As. Gideon Wise would hold the thin, creased papers carefully between his stained fingers, whispering the names of the subjects to himself, then folding the pages carefully away in a kitchen drawer. He never knew quite what to say to Joseph. Father and son ate their evening meal in silence, tucking their legs back onto the bars of their chairs like mirror images of each other.

When he finished school Joseph was given a scholarship for board and tuition at the university. He arrived knowing no-one, distanced from his father, feeling as though he had been lifted up out of his life and dropped into another world. He walked around the university, running his hands over the curved stone pillars and marvelling at the way the ivy made climbing patterns over the arts building. He stared at himself in the darkening windows of lecture halls and realised that he did not have to remain a workman's son. He had won passage out of his father's world and he never looked back.

Joseph was only nineteen when Aurel Stein and his desert took their hold on him. He sat at the back of a lecture theatre and listened to a man with a foreign accent speak about the way sand dunes moved across a desert plain. Stein's hands made sweeps and arcs to illustrate the rolling movement and Joseph could feel his passion move through the air.

Stein had been transplanted to Australia only months before Joseph met him. I couldn't understand this antipodean exile and imagined some disgrace, some fall from favour in the academy to see him so gracelessly turned out. But it wasn't that way at all, Joseph tells me. They were horrified when Stein left for Australia and tried to convince him not to throw his career away. There was no disgrace, only the love of a woman that brought him here.

What did he think, this German intellectual, when he was deposited in a town between the sea and the river with only one major university and no archaeology department to speak of? What did he think of the searing summer air and the stringy peppermint trees?

The woman left him after a few years but Stein stayed. How he had persuaded the university to set up a sinology department no-one knew, but he did. And it was there that my husband fell under his spell, that his love for China began.

In the dim light of the bookshop Ken Tiger narrates great distances for me. He takes me back to war-time Shanghai, to Ada, her life and her days. I sit by his chair and travel beside him on these journeys, but he never tells me anything about himself.

'Where do you come from, Ken?'

He turns his face towards me. It is late afternoon and the sun is in his eyes. In so many ways he is a shadow to me, a sketchy outline of a man. I need to firm him up if I want to see Ada Lang more clearly. I need to know who he is if I want to know who he loved. I lean towards him and he starts to speak.

'Every time I see a peasant fresh from the country I think

that he might be me. Me, but in a different life.'

If he had not met Ada Lang.

Ken Tiger was fifteen years old when he came to Shanghai. He had left his small village in Pudong with one change of clothes, a handful of coins and a slim-handled knife. It becomes a fiction, a legend, this childhood village, this journey. Later, when he is rich and well known, he will talk about naked children playing in unpaved streets, the water running between their feet red and filled with clay. *Shanghai, Shanghai*. Even the syllables have the sound of possibility.

There was the lurch of a small junk in the river, the glow of lamps over dark water and then the boy realised that he was surrounded by the city. It is a place of quick and easy riches, of uneasy fluidity, of invention and reinvention. A city of underworld societies, glamorous women, fabulous wealth and the sickly curl of smoke from opium dens. It is a story to frighten and enthral.

The boy's first image, his strongest memory: the chanting of the coolies as they laboured on the dock. The ever-present song of the Orient. The lines of men bent under back-breaking loads, their feet firm and sure on narrow planks. In all his years in the city this sound will haunt him, the singing beginning before first light and ending only after dusk. It will become for him the sound of all he will never let himself become.

A month in the city, his young heart still brimful with the dirge of slaves, he finds himself a student in a school for thieves. The school is in a room above a brothel on Foochow Road. At night the street is full of women, standing in the circle of a street lamp, within the shadow of a doorway, beckoning from the darkness of an alleyway.

As he climbs the stairs they laugh and call to him, the inflections of their voices sonorous and sweet.

The boys receive their training on life-sized straw dolls. The dolls are dressed in garments covered with small bells which ring at the slightest motion. A skilled pickpocket should be able to slip his hand into a coat without the slightest pressure, to slide his small knife through thick fabric to reach a pocket without ever being detected. It is a trade that suits the city, this repertoire of shadowy movements.

Like a Dickens' novel, it is at the school of thieves that the boy meets his benefactor. Du Yue-sheng was a legend more than he was a man. Opium, brothels, gold-smuggling, gun-running, slave-trading and hired killers. There was nothing, it was said, that he did not have a hand in. Du was a romance, a myth. He charmed the French police and was elected to the French Municipal Council. The Chinese loved him because he spread his hand across the city and made them believe that it was theirs for the taking. Thus the greatest criminal that China has ever produced became the centre of Shanghai.

He was a man of superstitions. His charmed fortune was due, he believed, to the dried heads of monkeys that were always fixed to the backs of his long gowns. Early in his life a fortune teller had told him that great wealth and long life would be his only if the head of a monkey reposed always in the middle of his back. If he failed to follow the soothsayer's advice then he could expect to meet a violent death. A knife blade, she said, between the ribs. Or a silk cloth, tight around the throat.

He was a man who believed in omens, who knew that ordinary facts, crowding tightly along the thread of reality, mask the contraband of hidden meanings and secret desires.

The day before Christmas Clarissa and I are sitting at her kitchen table, a pot of coffee between us. Through the window we are watching Geoffrey Ray setting off at a slow jog into the rainy afternoon. His hair is already wet and glossed flat to his head and he looks large and gingery. Clarissa holds her cup close to her face, letting the steam rise up to her skin.

'Good old Geoffrey,' she says absently. 'His bloody running.'

It's been raining for days. At dawn, through the night, an endless quiet breath. It hisses softly, casting an endless mist, blotting things out.

Clarissa is telling me about a prominent figure at the Hong Kong Club whose wife left him for another man.

'Anyway these are very well-known people and the whole thing was very public. The man who was left was completely devastated, and then he met this younger woman, who's a writer too actually, a journalist I think, and she got pregnant.'

She leans across the table as she speaks. Sometimes I think she is like a ripple of energy, with her mobile face and her various expressions.

'She had the baby,' Clarissa continues, 'so this guy has been left by his wife and publicly humiliated and suddenly at the age of fifty-five he's got this little baby and his whole life has changed.'

'And he's happy?'

'Yes, yes! He's stopped being this tragic figure and now he's just a doting father. He's radiant. He loves that child. And everyone says, "What a story, how wonderful."'

Clarissa loves telling stories. She has a showman's flair for delivery, withholding the key piece of information until precisely the right moment. I want to ask her for a story that can save you when you have become stupid with sadness. When the part of your mind that used to be able to grasp a narrative curve has suddenly dissolved. A soft, sinking tiredness overwhelms me and I push my hands through my hair. I feel like I have been disassembled. That I have given my life to someone who would think nothing of dropping it.

I remember something a friend once said to me when her second husband left her. The end of her first marriage had devastated her and she had been shattered for years. When I heard the news of the ruin of this second relationship, I rushed to see her. We sat in her garden and she brought me a cup of quince tea and sat there very quietly, her cat thrusting its head up against her palm as she stroked it.

'I don't think I have it in me any more to be destroyed by a man,' she said to me.

I want a place that can't be made dangerous or dark. Where a life can't be disfigured by love.

Clarissa stands behind me and puts her hands on my shoulders. I can feel her fingers kneading the sharp knobs of bone, the skin sliding over the flesh. She rests her hand on the back of my neck.

'Come to midnight mass with me tonight. I know you don't believe in it,' she says. 'I don't really either, but I always go.'

Clarissa often speaks about religion. Not about faith, or any kind of god, but the shape it makes around her life. 'The Anglicans are so dull,' she says. '"The bland leading the bland", my father used to say.'

I repeated this to Joseph once, during one of our increasingly rare dinners together, thinking to entertain him. I looked at him to see if he would laugh.

'Oh spare me Clarissa Ray's witticisms,' he said, pushing his chair back from the table. He was so busy now that he would go back to his office as soon as he had eaten, not coming home until long after I was asleep.

On the way to the church, Clarissa tells me how she used to go to mass with her mother and sister. Wherever they were in the world, the three of them would find a church on Christmas Eve and kneel at the back, joining in with the hymns.

The church is full of women. These are the Filipina amahs, the maids and the cooks who live in tiny rooms off kitchens in all the big houses on the Peak. Every white family has a dark-eyed amah to look after the children. You see them on the streets, pushing a stroller with a blond child. Their own children are back in the Philippines with a grandmother or a sister. The money they send back can support the whole family. Sometimes they don't go home for years.

On Sundays they are free and they congregate in the square off Chater Road. They bring their own food, packed neatly into straw baskets, and tin thermoses of tea. There are no men or children. The square sounds like an aviary, the high chattering voices rising up into the air like singing. Some of the amahs smoke sweet cigarettes. They all wear silver crosses around their necks.

The Ray's amah is called Flor and she is small and very

dark. 'A touch of the tarbrush there,' Geoffrey Ray once laughed. She wears print dresses and smiles shyly, showing shockingly brown teeth. Once I asked her about her family in the Philippines and she proffered a photograph of two small girls posing formally in pink taffeta dresses.

'We don't really need Flor any more,' Clarissa says. 'The children are old enough. But I feel sorry for the poor girl. She can always help in the kitchen I suppose.'

During mass I hear the soft sounds of weeping. I look around and see that nearly all the women are crying quietly, their heads bent over prayer books, an arm around a friend's waist. They all look so young. Neon signs on the street cast their light through the windows of the church. I wonder if they are thinking of the villages at home, the children and the mothers, the smells of their own food and songs in their language.

Beside me Clarissa finds the page in the hymn book and sings in a clear strong voice. After the mass is over she kisses me on the cheek. 'Merry Christmas, sweetheart.' *Sweetheart.* For me it's a tender name for a lover. Or a daughter.

Back at the apartment I sit for a long time with my notebook open in front of me.

In Perth when he was not teaching classes or in the library with Stein poring over old texts, Joseph would meet me in a cafe by the sea. He doesn't love the sea like I do. For him, the waterless swells of sand and rock. In the desert the dunes move like waves, he tells me. They have a life of their own. The great dunes, driven by desert winds, are marching diagonally towards the southern oases. Inch by inch, the desert moves. In the oasis towns they are constantly fighting back the desert. Over coffee he would tell me about elaborate systems of nets and plantings imported from the Alps.

'Like a seawall,' I said.

'Yes. In a way.'

'Will you take me there one day?'

He leaned over and cupped his hand around my chin. 'God, I love your face.'

It began in this cafe by the sea. We had worked in such close proximity at the university for more than two years. Always the polite greeting in the mornings, the proffered cups of tea, the nods in the corridor. And then that postcard from the desert.

The week after he came back from his field trip he knocked on my door. 'It's too hot to work. I need a beer.' I was sitting at my desk by the window and I turned and stared at this man leaning in the doorframe.

I slipped my feet into my shoes and picked up my bag. 'I know a place by the sea,' I said.

In the cafe he leaned towards me and ran a finger along my collarbone.

Later comes the body. The body is soft, thin, not lacking in muscle. We would lie there under the slow flickering of the ceiling fan and I would run my fingers over the strange lines of his shoulders, his arms, the curves and dips of his chest. I would trace the spirals of soft hairs on his stomach and at the base of his neck. We held each other loosely, the flesh softened and merged under the dripping blue heat of those early days, moisture forming in the place beneath the collarbone.

The first time he drew me to him I could smell the sun

on him and the fresh clean scent of soap. His body was all lines and curves, the flesh bracing against bone, the arms strong, the chest flecked with dark hair.

I liked to lay my cheek against the smooth upper reaches of his arm, to sleep against the warm smell of him. To wake submerged in the muskiness of flesh.

Lying awake in the heat of the summer nights, I told him stories. About my life before I met him, my childhood, my mother's house on the other side of the country. *The Cedars*. The farmhouse that her grandfather built and was supposed to come down to the sons through the generations. She was only a daughter but in the end she was the only one left to wipe the spittle from her father's chin when he lay dying. When she married she insisted the house be kept in her name. Perhaps she already saw something unreliable in my father, something not entirely to be trusted.

I told him about the stands of red cedar trees that give the house its name. The bark of the red cedar is so drenched with sap that when pulled off it drips with heavy liquid. When it's sawn the scent of the wood rises like incense to the nostrils, sharp and pungent. The eyes smart when a chip is held to the face. In the country, women sew the sawdust into pockets of calico to save their clothes from moths and silverfish. My mother put small packages in every dresser. Shaken from the drawer, my clothes always held the sharp smell of fresh wood.

The summer evenings when the sky holds the light for hours. The sea outside. The long straight lines of sky and water and horizon. In the bedroom there is light from the sea, a pure, dusk-blue light which falls slantwise through the blinds. We lie there without words. He slides his open palm along my back. *Ah the back*, he says, *the thinking man's breasts.*

These are the times when he is loose and expansive, when he will tell me things about himself. About his family.

In the beginning he only admitted them to me as a catalogue of names. He would not relinquish them any further. There was his father Gideon, his dead mother Hannah. The family home was on the other side of the river. 'The wrong side,' Joseph laughed.

When Joseph was small the suburb was still new, just a cluster of houses with the bush at its back. In some places the new roads gave way to dirty sand. Trucks came to seal them and the smell of tar seeped into hot kitchens. All the houses were identical, squat brick boxes set on large dusty blocks. In summer the sandfleas and the flies could drive you mad.

His mother moved the hose over the patchy lawn, the water running away into the sand. With no car, there was nothing for her to do all day but sweep and clean. His father laid out a vegetable patch for her at the bottom of the garden, with tomatoes and a row of corn. But she wasn't a woman like my mother. She didn't have efficient country ways and in summer the tomatoes fell and lay drying in the yellow grass.

Joseph's father is a mechanic. He can lean into a car's engine and listen to the motor as if it was something living and precious. It's the same listening pose of a mother bending over a sleeping, soft-breathing child. He's a man who knows how to make machines work.

Once, between the pages of a book, I found a snap someone had taken of Joseph's parents in front of the house. They are leaning against a railing, tilting slightly away from each other. Both look guarded and somewhat ill at ease. His father is tall and angular in his work overalls, his eyes creased in the sunlight. His mother is wearing a pale dress and the light has drained all the colour out of her. Only her hair is dark and springy. A year later she would die, swiftly and quietly. It was 1970 and they didn't know what to do about cancer.

Joseph was faintly ashamed of his father. All day Gideon worked at a garage tucked in between two warehouses on the outskirts of the city. Every morning from dawn, bent over the engines of cars. In the garage the men go for hours without speaking, uninterested in anything outside the focus of their world of machines. Their fingers move instinctively, expertly, separating a wire, tightening a bolt. In the afternoons they stand in the paved yard, shuffling their feet and sharing coffee from a thermos.

'Tell me about your father,' I asked Joseph in the early days, when all I knew of him was his impossible name. Gideon.

We were up on the high grass banks above the ocean, eating fish and chips from the paper, licking the grease from our fingers. It was early evening and the water was slapping at the shore. The last swimmers were coming up from the beach, clutching towels around their shoulders and stamping the sand loose from their feet. We had brought wine, sweet and white, and late-summer figs from my garden.

Joseph was sitting behind me on the picnic rug, my back curled into his chest. I could feel the firmness of his ribs against my shoulders and I tried not to lean too heavily against him. When he spoke, his chest moved behind me.

When Joseph was small the things he hated most about his father were his personal habits. His smells and noises. The faint layer of oil and petrol he left behind him, the steamy smell of Radox and shaving cream in the bathroom, his loud rumbling coughs in the night.

He knew that his father had had another life, a secret life. When he was young he had worked in the mines up north, had lived in a miner's hut on a red sprawl of dust. A black-and-white photograph shows him standing in a row of dirt-streaked men, the lights on their helmets refracting the camera's flash.

Every day he would climb down into the dank, slippery

darkness, feeling the weight of the whole earth above him. They had all imagined the rock caving in, heaving them under in a dusty death. Down there the air was always dense and warm. By midday the men would be dripping in sweat, the stale smell of them cloying and sharp against the deeper smell of the earth. The only sound was the shattering and splintering of rock, the clatter of the jackhammer and the muffled blast of dynamite. Every blow of the pick against rock shuddered through the body like an electrical charge.

Joseph once showed me a remarkable photograph. It was from a newspaper clipping. An image of his father standing at the entrance to a mine shaft holding a birdcage. The canary is a limp smudge on the floor of the cage. The picture was originally attached to an article about the poor air quality in the mines, the dangers to the men. But the story has been cut away and all that remains is a disembodied picture of a serious man holding a dead bird.

'I didn't think they used canaries that recently,' I said.

'They didn't. They staged the whole photo for dramatic effect. Some smart journo's idea.'

'And then what? Why did he leave the mines?'

'Oh …'

'Didn't he meet your mother at a hotel in Fremantle? Was she very beautiful?'

I'm dying for him to dramatise his stories for me, to turn them into a cohesive narrative. But he's always laconic about the past.

'He left the mines when he was about thirty I suppose and moved down to the city and became a mechanic. Then he caught sight of my mother serving beer.'

'And he was transfixed?'

'I don't think my father's ever been *transfixed* by anything in his life. He probably just thought she might be a good prospect.'

'Hannah.' I roll his mother's name around my tongue. 'It's a good Jewish name.'

'Well, they had a good Catholic courtship, a nice church wedding and me a year later.'

I can't fit his father's life into such a dry outline. I sit up at my desk while Joseph sleeps in the room behind me and I write it down. I lay out my bare bones and move them around until I've got some sort of cohesive skeleton.

In one version, the story turns on a death.

When the miners find impassable walls of rock they send the dynamiters down the tunnel to dig sticks of explosive into fissures in the rock. The men wait in hollowed-out caverns for the dim roar of shattering rock, eating slabs of fruitcake their wives have wrapped in foil. Gideon crouches on his heels, leaning back against the cold shale rock. His shift is over in an hour and he's thinking about the cafe he'll stop at on the way home, the one where the waitress knows that he doesn't want to talk, just wants a coffee and a steak and a smoke.

And then a blast in the deeper darkness that's too loud, too close. One misjudged charge and the rock wall comes in on them. Later, when he lives in a city by the ocean, he'll say it looked like a great wave crashing over them. A wave with the fierce deadliness of shattering rock. Knocked flat on his back, at the furthest end from the blast, Gideon can hear the wails and groans of men. In the darkness, the flowing blood looks black.

After the rescues, after the men have been dragged out half-dead and missing arms and legs, and after the funerals and the lowering of eleven coffins with the whole town turned out to throw a handful of dirt onto the shiny, disappearing wood, Gideon Wise walked home, took off his miner's boots and left the railway town forever.

Or perhaps the ending is less easily marked. Perhaps, in some moment, hacking into rock, feeling the blows jar into his shoulders, his skull, he loses faith in the earth. He feels a gurgling like waterfalls in his chest and starts to feel that he is down too deep, that the rock pressing down on him can no longer be trusted.

That day he steps out from underground for the last time, packs up his few belongings and catches the train south to Perth.

Years later he will try, but fail, to tell his son that his one happiest moment was standing on the desert plain in his filthy boots. The pleasure of the glare of sun and sky, the sense of himself as a man again after all those years hunched underground.

Gideon Wise emerged from the mines a silent man, unused to the habits of cities and withdrawn from the people around him. He landed on the docks at Fremantle and stood there breathing everything in. The fast evaporation of night and the grey dawn air, the huddles of men having the first smoko of the day, stamping their feet in the cold. The air smells of brine and machinery. Beyond the sheds the ships sit huge and silent in the early light.

New machines have just arrived. Gleaming monsters of cranes with their stiff arms stretching out across the harbour. They need drivers and men who know how to service them and within the week Gideon has a job. Not as a lumper, or a wharfie, but a crane driver. He likes to feel that he is an extension of a machine, the crane's long arm reaching out of his body into the air. The power of it, the precision.

He rented a room at the dark end of an upstairs corridor in a boarding house on High Street. The heavy front door opens onto what the landlady called the parlour. There were grimy windows looking over the street, a blackened paraffin stove, a lino table. The faint smell of frying oil hangs in the hallway. Across the road was Watsonia's famous Number Four Shop.

Gideon met Hannah in the first week of his arrival in Fremantle. When the wharf workers finished for the day they would walk through the West End to the Orient Hotel on Henry Street and sit in the comforting gloom of the front bar. She was busy at the bar, pouring beers, bringing out counter meals from the poky kitchen behind her. Every few minutes she would brush her hair out of her eyes with the back of her hand.

When there was a lull, Hannah would lean on the counter and watch the men from the wharf. She liked the way men were with each other, the names they had for each other. *Brooksie. Hendo. Paddo. Italy.* She listens to their jokes and the stories they recite. To the poetry of spare, masculine speech.

She had come from Melbourne to escape a house of women. Five younger sisters and a flustered, overbearing mother. An aunt from her dead father's side ran the Orient Hotel and Hannah got board and lodging in return for serving at the bar and helping to clean the rooms. The tips were enough for the occasional trip to the pictures. After Melbourne, this port city, perched on the furthest edge of the country, felt like a frontier town.

Gideon would watch her movements, the competent sweep of the cloth across the counter, the clever look on her face as she added up bills, the way her fingers tap-tapped on the counter in time to the music. When she bent forward he always wanted to reach over and run his fingers through her curly hair. To her he was a man who seemed completely self-sufficient. He had revealed nothing, not even his name, just the silver coin left on the counter every day, gleaming in the dim light.

Every night after the bar closed, Hannah sat up at the table in her bedroom, hunched over in the small circle of the night light and read romance novels. She read lustily about square-jawed men with impossible names and Spanish galleons and women framed in lace and rose-coloured silk. Novels filled with clear stories and conclusions. She fell asleep smiling dreamily, her body full of other lives.

After a month Gideon asked her to dinner at the Capri, down the road on South Terrace. It's still there, wedged in between the trendy coffee shops, with its red-checkered tablecloths and the faded posters of Sicily on the walls. The menu was Italian: minestrone soup, scallopine, little gelato peaches.

Hannah sits across from him, her head tilted quizzically to one side as if she is trying to read him and he thinks that with her slim face and olive skin and gleaming hair she is the most beautiful woman he has ever seen. A string of coral beads rolls against her neck. Later, when he kisses her, her lips feel cool and smooth.

These were days when it was always summer. Steam trains rolled in and out of Fremantle Station bringing bales of wool, men still dusty from the desert, city girls, sequinned and gauzy. Union meetings were held secretly in warehouses on the docks, whisky shared from hipflasks, all of them trespassing. The Workers Clubs were always full, wiry children roamed the streets and on Saturday nights wild music drifted down from the Italian Club.

On Sundays they were all free. The men walked down to South Beach, towels slung over their shoulders. On the sand they stripped down to shorts, pushing and splashing each other, swimming in clusters close to the shore. Lying afterwards on the sand, hair plastered to their skulls, eyes screwed tightly shut against the sun, a radio playing somewhere in the distance.

Gideon lay there, not wanting to speak, letting the sun wash over him, released from a week of work. Soon he would have Hannah in his arms, sit with her in the dark closeness of the picture hall, leaning in for a kiss in the minutes of blackness when the projectionist changed the reels. Then they would walk over to Cicerellos where they would sit on warm benches and throw chips to the gulls, Hannah telling him in her clear voice the story of the book she was reading.

Later he will strain to remember every detail of those evenings. Hannah licking salt from her fingers and leaning forward eagerly to tell him long complicated narratives of journeying heroes and their returns, women swept up by pirates and revenges cleverly exacted. He will come back to those nights again and again, like a small pool of light in a great darkness. For him, they will become the long-remembered words of an old song, the page he always goes back to.

This is all my romance, of course. I spin these stories out of the scraps of himself that Joseph offers me. Perhaps if I create a history for him, if I can imagine the places he has come from, then I will feel as if I know him.

My thoughts keep turning back to Ada Lang. Did she look out at her Chinese city of exile and think that its heart must lie somewhere? Was she looking for some kind of largeness, some extension of herself?

She lost sight of herself because there was no-one to pull taut the line that connected her past to her present. Loosened, the thread grew slack and she felt herself adrift, a pliable self that might be altered by any encounter.

Ada Lang found work in a silk factory. Shanghai is a city of silk. From the shops on Nanking Road billow every type of crepe de Chine, silk gauze, silk chiffon, pongee and Shandong silks and fine silk brocades woven with emblems like the everlasting knot and the lotus. Ada has watched the clerks in long grey gowns pull down bolt after bolt of silk, shaking out the material in glistening waves.

The production of silk requires small and nimble fingers. When she applied for the position the foreman examined Ada's hands carefully, the fine fingers, the traceries of blood beneath the surface, the purple veins rearing up like rivers.

To make silk the web must be removed from the soft cocoon of the silkworm. One silk thread requires the web from six cocoons. Each morning the women and children take their places opposite each other in reeling sheds lined with metal benches. The children sit before basins of boiling water and put their hands into the almost-scalding water, stir the cocoons, then pass the soaked cocoon over to another tray of water in front of the women. The job of the women is to join the silken webs together and pass them through pulleys to winding-frames. Steam fills the shed and the women drip with sweat, their grey overalls damp and heavy. A pungent stench from the dead cocoons fills the room. Tightly swaddled babies lie asleep under the reeling drums behind their mothers' backs.

Together the women spend their days spinning out the fine weave of thread so soft it feels like a butterfly's wing against the skin. The transparent silken webs from the cocoon are so light that they cling to the women's hair, to their clothes, their cheeks. In the dim light of the shed the women are diaphanous, silken.

Ada took her place between the Chinese women, her

hands pale and chalky between tones of olive and caramel. They could have been cruel to her. She was not one of them, with her strange hair and her foreign language. They could have been unkind but they were not. Perhaps they sensed in her some spectacular self, some legend undeciphered. They gathered her up with a quiet, protective tenderness, touched her hair shyly and with baffled awe. They taught her fragments of their language and brought her cakes of cassia petals, lotus seeds and Siamese oranges.

Later, when Lord Kadoorie finds her, he will say that he saw the women as oriental sentries, guarding her for him until he could come and take her away.

One morning I walk across the courtyard to the Faculty of Arts. Students stare silently at me as I pass them. I remember Joseph telling me that what made Hong Kong so different from other British colonies was the refusal of the Chinese to behave like good colonial subjects. They were nothing like the naïve Africans or the smiling Malays. They were self-sufficient and as indifferent as they could be to the British. Every single one of them had been brought up in the conviction that every Chinese ever born was superior to every foreigner.

Inside the archaeology building the corridors are cool and quiet. They smell of old linoleum and dust. The windows look out onto squares of white sky. People stare at me from open doors. I don't see any women.

I walk past a glass-walled library, a tiny kitchenette where two men are talking. I can hear the sound of my own footsteps. Then men's voices stop and they stare at me. I smile but they keep staring blankly. Sometimes I think that these people will always be inaccessible to me. Once I told Joseph that I thought they deliberately conspired to fulfil all the western clichés about them, about their inscrutability.

Joseph's office is very small and bare. There is a long table against the window and some straight-backed chairs. The desk is very empty, there are only neat piles of books. There are no pictures on the walls, no photographs, just the maps of his desert. Does he really live such an ordered life?

I think that if for me, life is a slow amassing of treasures, of sparkling red crystal and plates of Mexican blue, of lino prints and white jugs of narcissus, for Joseph it is a gradual stripping bare. A slow reduction to order and sparseness. A spare, unpainted room, neat rows of books, quiet, uncluttered hours.

I search the room for signs of him. There's an electric kettle and a box of the green tea he likes on top of a small cabinet. I fill the kettle and stand by the window while I wait for the water to boil. The room is flooded with hazy light over the wooden furniture. I sit at his desk with my cup of tea, my hands folded on the desk in front of me.

I stare at the map of China pinned to the bare whitewashed wall.

What am I doing here?

Ken Tiger has fallen in his shop by the square. The woman who sells jackfruit tells me. He had a moment of blackness, a flare of dizziness and fell heavily. They took him to the Chinese hospital.

In the taxi on the way to the hospital I think about the fragility of bone, the sickening sound of a snapping wrist.

The ward where they have put him is crowded and bleak. People groan and sigh around him. The man in the next bed yells out incoherently. The nurses are brisk and unsympathetic.

Against the hospital whiteness Ken Tiger looks tired and small. I've brought him a packet of tea. An oolong. He smiles as I fuss with hot water, paper cups. It's nothing, he says, collarbones heal, the pain's not so bad. He shifts against the pillow and I see him wince. I reach over and stroke his arm. I read once that human touch can heal, that after all the medicines in the world it's flesh against flesh that we need. Some of the women here go on charity trips to orphanages. *Just to hold the babies*, they say. Just so they can feel arms around them. Ken Tiger stays very still and quiet and I go on stroking his arm. People can forget what touch is.

After a while I ask him to tell me about Victor Kadoorie. Lord Kadoorie, the man who married Ada, plucking her from anonymous poverty. I know him as a stern figure of a man, a handsome portrait on the wall at the Hong Kong Club, a name that means unimaginable wealth. I know there's more to him. There must be a story behind the legend.

Victor Kadoorie, he says, was almost English. He fought for England in the war. He had been injured in service and walked with a slight limp. He had been to Cambridge and so had his father before him but it was never quite enough. Once when he was very young he had joined in a dinner party conversation about the best route home. A woman had cut in unkindly. 'Don't you go by camel?' she had asked.

It didn't matter though, says Ken Tiger, because before long he was richer than any of them. He won them over in the end.

Victor Kadoorie. There he is, a giant of a man, as ambitious as the empire itself. A dream of Shanghai. He was a man from the desert, from the sun. He should have been draped in rich fabrics and gazing out across curving sands and spindly minarets. Instead he was sent away to school in England.

Long after he is rich and successful he will surely remember the bitter cold of that first English winter. He will remember the whole world coloured brown and grey and the light soft and dull, not like the light of India. In those first weeks he was convinced that they had brought him to the wrong place, that the ship had lost its way during the long weeks at sea. This could not be the England he knew from the pages of his books. That England was green and lush and consisted of gentle plains and castles with strange and wonderful histories. It was a land of soldiers and kings, of conquerors and sweeping skirts, high tea served from glass-thin china at every far outpost of his Indian childhood. It was not this cold world of drizzling rain and white skies.

The cold settled in his bones and rattled him with its relentless *realness* until he felt India to be an insubstantial dream and himself nationless. He thought of his mother and the spices she chewed to sweeten her breath. When she had kissed him goodbye at the dock he had felt her mouth musky and warm against his cheek. Now, in his dormitory world, the shape and the smell of her seemed like something from a dream and he became stricken by the idea that he had imagined his mother. The calico pockets of cloves she had pressed into the corners of his trunk to scent his clothes seemed like illicit mementoes from some dream kingdom.

He lay shivering in bed and watched the charwoman lighting the fire with lumps of coal. The sticks crackled and hissed for a long time before the flames shot up. Under the blankets he pressed a sachet of cloves to his face.

In the years to come he succeeded at everything he turned his hand to. In England he wore a loose suit and charmed well-born ladies. He came out with top marks in all his classes at Cambridge and played polo with the boys who had once taunted him. He rarely talked about his past or his devoutly Jewish, old-world mother.

When his education was finished he boarded another ship, not back to Bombay, but to Shanghai to set up a Chinese office for the family company. In Shanghai he expanded the company's interests into real estate, hotels, rubber plantations, merchant banks. He was the only man to win seats, simultaneously, on the Municipal Councils of the French Concession and the British Settlement. Everything he touched turned to gold.

It is a fine morning. The harbour is full of ships and life. The very world pours through this port. There are clippers from London, ships with French and American flags, lines of junks all the way from Annam. Victor Kadoorie is standing on the dock, his pipe in hand, watching the coolies unload his ships. The dock is cluttered with crates and boxes. Bare-chested men in grass Hupeh hats run up and down planks from the boats and sweating foremen tick off shipments on long lists.

These are his favourite moments, the moments before his endless round of meetings and negotiations and tiffin at the club. Before going to his office on the Bund he loves to come and watch the life of the harbour. He leans on a rail in the sun, drawing on his pipe and watching the ships. The men below tip their hats to him, sometimes bringing up a list for him to inspect.

On these shining Chinese mornings it is the small boy trying desperately to summon his mother from the smell of cloves who is the fictitious character, the first cold days in England the shadowy dream.

On the train into Kowloon I watch a young mother and her baby. The woman is holding the child on her lap and staring adoringly into her face as if she was some astounding gift, the loveliest thing ever to have existed. The baby stares up at her mother with a steady, black-eyed gaze, waving her arms up and down. For long minutes, the circuit of their gaze is unbroken. Mother and child.

Two years ago there was going to be a child between Joseph and me. I knew at once that I was pregnant. I had listened to enough conversations about aching breasts and rising nausea. I lay in bed sour-mouthed in the mornings and thought about the soft stretch of skin that crowns an infant's skull. My breasts swelled and I tried to imagine the feel of a tiny mouth suckling, the firm wet pressure of it.

It was winter and when I went out walking the sea was slick and grey. Every day it was dark earlier and the path above the beach was empty in the late afternoons. Joseph was away in Melbourne, guest-lecturing for a month at the university there. When he wasn't teaching he was reading, trying to cram in as much research as he could. He called me every evening but I couldn't form my mouth around the words to tell him.

We had not planned for it, had never even discussed the question of children. I had always assumed that Joseph didn't want children, that fatherhood would only be a distraction from his work. I thought he might see my pregnancy as an inconvenience. Every evening I put off telling him because I thought he might offer me a sensible catalogue of reasons against having this child. We weren't exactly young any more, both of our careers were demanding, we weren't really prepared at this stage of the game to raise a child. What I was scared of was the prospect of his displeasure.

In the afternoons I sat in the chair by the window, the cat curled against my belly. This baby would be born under a clear summer sky. She would have long fingers, her father's curls. She would grow up by the sea, held between her parents in the waves. Sometimes I would fall asleep to the sound of the waves and the cat's insistent purring.

In my dream Joseph is standing above me, the square of his shoulders framed by the window. There is a scent of rain and distant thunder. He slides to his knees and runs his fingers along my collarbone and down my body, brushing lightly over my breasts until his hands come to rest on the mound of my stomach. The skin is taut and translucent, the small creature curled inside wholly unimaginable. Joseph lowers his head and places it against the rise of my belly, his hair soft and curling against my skin. When I look down I can see the curve of a smile on his face. His eyes are closed.

Then the dream slides into an image of my mother sitting on the verandah of the farmhouse with my youngest brother held to her breast. She's alone and I can see vividly the exhaustion on her face and the way she stares out across the fields. Something that she once said to me: *you love your children, but they suck the life from you.*

The day that Joseph was due home from Melbourne, I woke up to find my legs slippery with blood. I stared down at the sheets for a long time, wondering where so much blood could have escaped from.

It had been dark for hours when Joseph arrived at the hospital. I had asked them to open the window and I could smell the rain, caught in a pocket of the wind. He came and sat on a low stool near the bed and leaned forward. He whispered my name and ran his fingers through my hair again and again. It was a gesture that he had often used in love.

My lips felt thick and dry. 'I'm sorry,' I said to him. It was the only thing I could think of to say. He stared down at me for a moment and then he pushed his face against my shoulder and wept. It was the first time I had ever seen him cry. I stroked his forehead, the way you might a feverish child, and he wept for a long time.

The blinds scratched against the windows and I could hear the swish of traffic from the freeway. 'Take me home,' I said.

Without a word, he wrapped the blanket tight around me, gathered me into his arms and carried me out of the hospital into the cold night. No-one tried to stop us.

Back at our house he lay beside me in bed and pressed my hand tight against his chest. In the morning he drew the curtains so that I wouldn't be woken by the sunlight.

After that night in the hospital we never spoke of it again.

The train lurches into the station. I am visiting Clarissa Ray at her house on the colony's hill station. On the Peak the air is cooler and thinner and the haze is never as heavy as it is in the city. You can fill your lungs with air. Sometimes in the afternoons, after the shopping, the eating, the talking, Clarissa's chauffeur will drive us up to her villa where we sit in wicker chairs and drink cold tea and stare out past the lawns, past the winding road down the mountain, to the view beyond.

Today Clarissa serves tea on the terrace, with saucers and a silver jug of milk. There is shortbread, thick and crumbling.

'Charlie Woo made it,' she says, smiling benevolently at the lanky houseboy. 'It's his specialty. The people before us taught him.'

At the far end of the garden two boys are burning the dead undergrowth, tossing armfuls of dry leaves onto a pyre. A trail of ashes and wavering smoke rises up against the sky and the thick, scorching heat of the flames drifts in waves across the grass. I can feel it against my legs, in my eyes.

The tea and the shortbread are for Mrs Experience Barrows. Joseph laughed when he heard her name, said that was just what the colony needed, another Victorian battleaxe. But she's an American, Mrs Barrows, from New Hebron in Vermont. She shows us a miniature landscape her daughter painted of the Green Mountains above the town. So lush they are, the Green Mountains, like you wouldn't believe. And the town. Every building on the main street is on the US Historical Register. It hasn't changed in a hundred years, New Hebron. If you look at the old photographs in the Historical Society you'd swear they had been taken yesterday.

Her house was on the Historical Register, of course. They had come, just last year, to fix a plaque over the door. There had been a party to celebrate, an old-fashioned barn dance, with everyone in costume and homemade cider and candied apples for the children. Of course, being on the register meant that you couldn't do anything to the house without permission. Not even change the colour, or the tiles on the roof. Her husband had wanted to put a swing set out the front, for the grandchildren, but that was out of the question. You weren't even supposed to park your car on the street. It was very important that the streetscape wasn't altered.

I ask why it is so important for everything to stay the same.

'Because it's our history. History's not just something you look at in the Historical Society you know.'

Clarissa says that she has been to Vermont, to see the colours in the fall.

'Yes. Leaf-peepers, we call you. People who just come to look at the foliage. New Hebron's packed with them in October. Columbus Day Weekend is like a circus.'

She tells us how, really, New Hebron wouldn't be there if it wasn't for her grandfather. It's all documented, right there in the Historical Society, how he saved twenty-seven old homes from being destroyed when they were flooding a dam north of the town. He dismantled them, every single one, from the curled cornices to the chimney pipes and put them all together again, right on Main Street. Some of the parts got mixed up though, and there were dreadful fights about which oak panelling belonged to which library and which lamp fixtures went with which house.

'Even now, they still argue about it,' she sighs, trailing a spoon through her tea.

'We should get going,' Clarissa says, standing up and slapping at a mosquito, leaving a smear of blood on her brown leg.

We are going to a Vietnamese slum, a great encampment between two bridges, to give handmade dolls to the children. It has been Mrs Experience Barrow's great project while here in the colony, the making of these dolls. The Arts and Crafts Society sewed them, over tea and sherries at the Club. 'The Stitch and Bitch Club,' Clarissa calls it. Still, I go along with her sometimes, embroidering a lopsided smile or stitching woollen braids to a cushiony head.

The Vietnamese have been swimming to Hong Kong in batches since the war, Clarissa tells me. Most of them die on the way over or are rounded up into refugee camps. The ones that slip through find work in the big houses or in the cafes and factories in the city. You can hire them for nearly nothing and they're good workers, better than the Filipinos.

The slum is a straggling mess of sheet metal and old cardboard lashed together with wire and bamboo poles. In some places more permanent huts of board and tin have been put up and rangy-looking dogs lie in the dust close to the walls. In the shade of one of the few stunted trees some women are squatting on the ground, their skirts hanging between their legs. There's a group of children playing in the full sun and they turn to stare at us as we walk through the makeshift chicken-wire gate.

Mrs Barrows knows what to do, she's used to orchestrating acts of mercy. When they were in Nigeria, she told us, she knitted Christmas stockings for every child in the village. She grabs a handful of dolls from the box Clarissa's driver is holding and walks towards the women under the tree.

'We've brought dolls for your children,' she says loudly and slowly, as if she were talking to small children. The women stare up at her, open-mouthed.

'It's a great honour for them to have white people come here,' she says to Clarissa and me. 'They're not used to it.'

The children take the dolls, shyly and suspiciously. Mrs Experience Barrows talks loudly to them as she hands out the bounty. 'My my, aren't you a pretty one. No pushing … manners, manners.'

A small boy sidles up to me, slips his hands into the folds of my dress and stares up at me curiously. His legs are wiry and knobby-kneed. He should be wearing school shorts, tearing around a playground with a soccer ball. Two little girls sit cross-legged in the dust at our feet, their new rag dolls clutched solemnly in their hands. At the edge of the crowd a girl of no more than seven or eight is holding a baby on her hip. She's got that universal mother's stance, legs planted wide, one hip pushed out to the side. The baby's head lolls sleepily against her skinny shoulder.

I don't know if I can take much more of this. I'd like to take them all home with me. It's hard to maintain any sort of composure. Then Clarissa moves slightly closer to me so that her shoulder leans against mine. I slip my arm through hers and we stand there together watching the children.

Later, back at Clarissa's house on the Peak, she pours glasses of white wine. I watch her hands, the solid lines of her brown wrists. Beyond her, through the bay window, I can see the garden boy working at the hedges. He flicks the shears back and forth with quick, deft movements. Even through the glass I can hear the swish and snap of metal against metal.

We are both silent. We are thinking of the faces of the children. Of their rheumy eyes and thin limbs. The exhausted-looking mothers.

Clarissa looks thoughtful. Sometimes there are confidences between us. Nothing whispered breathlessly, but there are words across a table.

'In India we had a maid who lived in the house. She was quite beautiful. Those women are all beautiful. The house was very pale. Lots of white and gauze netting and light wood. She used to wear very bright saris. It was nice just to look at her against all that paleness.

'But Geoffrey liked to do more than just look. He's

always liked the dark girls. The only doctors for the poor were at the Catholic Mission and they wouldn't give her an abortion.

'One day — I remember the day because I had just come back from the islands and it was pouring with rain — she walked all the way from the Mission hospital to the house. She had wrapped the baby in one of her saris. That's how she left it, in a tiny heap in the hallway. Just laid it down and slipped away.

'I found it when I came down for lunch. I thought someone had dropped a bundle of rags. When I picked it up it fitted so perfectly against my breast.'

She touches her breast absently, as if she was remembering a lost weight held there once.

'What did you do?'

'Found the mother. She said she couldn't take it. In the end she did, with a bit of money. Geoffrey saw to it. Sometimes I wonder what happened to them but you can't think about it.'

She pauses and plays with the pearls around her neck. 'You know, for one instant when I first saw the little thing there on the floor I thought I should keep it. Take it on. It was a pretty baby. A little girl. Geoffrey thought I was mad. And I probably was.'

She looks at me and for a minute I think she is about to cry. 'There was this moment. We had to keep it for the night while they looked for the mother. The cook made a bottle for it. It cried in the night and I thought it must be hungry but as soon as I picked it up it stopped. It just wanted to be held.'

As I'm walking home I'm thinking about the marks lovers always leave, about how, in the end, we all want someone to hold us.

We are eating lunch in a small fish restaurant. It's late and we're the only diners. Across the table Ken Tiger is rubbing his palms gently against his neck. Earlier I had been telling him about the seafood restaurants on the beach at home. I wanted, I had said, to eat fish within sight and sound of the sea.

So he brought me to this small fishing village on the edge of the China Sea. The main street drops away into the blueness of Deep Bay. The restaurant is on a wharf above long white peninsulas of shells. Discarded oyster shells, Ken Tiger tells me, bleached white by the sun. The little bay is full of fishing boats. Their nets gleam in the sun.

It's the first time we've been out together. After his days in the hospital he's happy to be outside. On the ferry here he had been silent, shading his eyes and looking back at Hong Kong Island.

Ken Tiger tells me this: In Shanghai impoverished intellectuals would write their autobiographies in chalk on the pavement and invite the charitable to lay money on the incident that particularly moved them.

I don't know why the story of Ada Lang has taken such a hold of me. I don't know why I want to spread out her life as if it was a story in chalk.

In Shanghai a prosperous businessman fell in love with a penniless Russian Jew. He plucked her from the ghetto and brought her to his grand house in the French quarter. He bought her jewels and fine clothes, placed servants at her disposal and gave her free rein over his money. It was a fairytale of Shanghai. He was entranced, it was said, by the strange red flare of her unusual hair.

It began with a length of silk.

Weighing a piece of silk in his hands Victor Kadoorie was struck by its fineness, by the sheer, breath-like shift of it. He thought that such silk could sell for a fortune in London and that afternoon he went to visit the place where it was made.

The factory owner, bowing and offering silent thanks to his gods, took him on a tour of the sheds where the silk was spun. It was there, in the crisscrossed sun filtering through the window grates, that he saw Ada.

She was standing in front of a tray of scalding water, her

fingers moving through the sodden whiteness of the cocoons. Strands of wispy silk clung to her hair and her dark apron. Her hair was loose and it blazed where the segmented sun fell on it. He stared at her and she looked back at him through the rows of women. She trailed her fingers through the water and regarded him with a clear, unblinking gaze.

Victor Kadoorie sent his proposal without ever having laid eyes on her again. Within the month they were married and he had brought her to his new house on Bubbling Well Road. I don't know if the Hakhams were invited to the wedding, if she cried when she kissed Naima goodbye. She took nothing with her from the house on Chusan Road.

The startling news of Victor Kadoorie's passion for Ada Lang spread all over the city. At parties, the women leaned together, their voices low.

'Why should he marry a refugee without a penny to her name when he could have any girl in Shanghai? He'll regret it, of course he will, he'll want someone in his own league.'

'And she so strange. With that way of half-closing her eyes and that blank look.'

'But pretty I suppose. In an odd way.'

Why did Victor Kadoorie marry Ada? Was it the hand of rescue across a darkening sea? Did he see something of her coiled concealments and dispossession and want to hold up a lantern for her? Perhaps he thought he could invade her past and refashion its story, bleach out her loss with the clear strong light of his world. Or thought, as lovers do, that he could stand guard over her and beat off her demons as they came at her out of the darkness.

And Ada? Once she had seen a Chinese wedding procession. The bride, dressed in red, sat concealed in a lacquer sedan chair carried by servants. Ada thought that the word marriage was a safe, enclosed space, a concealment in itself.

Every day I walk around the city. From the Kowloon Gardens I arc out into the street of birds, or towards the harbour. Sometimes I cross the square and drink tea with Ken Tiger. In the early mornings the day is clear and the gardens are rooms of green light but by afternoon the air is thick with cloud and the prickle of moisture.

I'm glad that the women were kind to Ada. I'd like the quiet solidarity of women. The rise and fall of voices, the hands among tea cups, the confidences, the shared women's knowledge. The loose arm flung around the shoulders. An embrace, no lover's bracing grip, but as encompassing.

My mother never had woman friends. She never

150 • Alice Nelson

exchanged confidences over a pot of tea. After her husband left there was the farm to run and children to feed. She didn't have time for scones and shortbread and dances at the town hall. She was not a soft mother-shape like the women who waited for their children at the school gate. If you tried to hug her she would submit stiffly, holding herself slightly away from you.

When I was small I shared a bed with her. She slept neatly on her side of the bed, her back turned to me. I used to lie awake and watch the even rise and fall of her shoulders. I would edge closer and closer to her until there were only inches between us. I hoped that she might turn towards me in her sleep, that I might feel the warm weight of her against me.

She didn't encourage girlfriends from school. I didn't have the sprigged Liberty dresses of the other girls and in any case, I was happy playing with my brothers in the far corner of the schoolyard.

I didn't learn about the intimacies that exist between women until I went to university. In the room adjoining mine was a Spanish woman, a film student. She had the name of a famous male artist. In the evenings she would come into my room and sit cross-legged in the armchair. I sat behind the trestle table I used as a writing desk in those days. We would tell each other stories. We didn't have hot chocolate but my friend always wore silk pyjamas.

She told me about her home at the foot of mountains so

high their peaks vanished into the clouds. She spoke of her mother's saints and her father's beery breath against her face. When she was six the mother had taken her saints and her lace mantilla and disappeared with an English tourist, leaving my friend and her younger sister with the beery father.

Leaning across the table she whispered about lovers. She was sleeping with one of her tutors and she told me about him, about the way he took her hand and slowly ran his tongue along her palm. His body, she said, was so contained and delicately proportioned. Then she asked me about the man I was seeing. Did he have a beautiful penis, she asked me. I had never spoken like this with another woman, never narrated myself breathily. It was a kind of guilty pleasure.

When she spoke I watched her with a lover's interest. I noticed the way her eyes grew large when she was animated, the humorous twist of her mouth, the paleness of the secret flesh of her stomach that showed between the gaps of her pyjama top.

When the tutor abandoned her she came pounding into my room and climbed into bed with me. I put my arms around her and she wept heavily, her tears leaving great hot patches on my shirt. Her whole body shuddered and she looked like a small girl. I stroked her hair and whispered to her and eventually she fell asleep. I wanted to claim her suffering as my own special pain. I didn't want to offer lukewarm consolation, only the hot weight of shared anguish.

Eventually she married a rich Mexican architect and moved to Mexico with him.

Years later I saw a film she had made. It was all there, the childhood she had narrated on those late whispery nights. There were her mountains, her terracotta-hued village and her own small shape watching her mother drive away. She had caught all the dismal horror and the moments of unexpected tenderness with the beery father. She had narrated herself more successfully than I ever could.

I'd like to have my Spanish friend here now. I'd put her in the armchair across from me, a pot of tea between us, and I'd read my pages about Ada Lang to her. I can see her now, closing her eyes and nodding seriously as I read, frowning at a clumsy line or a slip in the story.

Yes, that's the place I'd like to be. In the landscape of someone else's past, between the closed pages of the history book.

I might tell her my own story too, if only it would stay still. If only it would stop swerving and take a shape I can make into a narrative. Then maybe I could find a way to explain us all.

When I get home from my walk there's a letter from Joseph. It's propped up against the empty fruit bowl. He's had to go back to the desert unexpectedly. Something has come up. I shouldn't expect him before the end of the week. I walk from one side of the room to the other. Wall to wall, it's only six small steps.

I think of Joseph, already on the road, rubbing his jaw and squinting into the sun. Happy to be away from the university, from politics, from me. He once told me that after a day in the desert he no longer thought about anything. One day and he had moved into the world of shifting dunes and buried cities. In a way I suppose it's like the enclosure of the writer's trance, that sweet removal from the world.

The desert is a world of men. There's a particular tradition for them to operate in. Hard drinking, long days, the quick silence of the nights. Wives at home, books and Archaeological Society meetings. I've read the monographs, sat in dim church halls listening to lectures on discoveries made in the desert. There's never any mention in these lectures of human behaviour, of the soft sweet eyes of the women who sell water in the oasis towns, of the way that a man sometimes feels a slippage in his mind after days out in the desert. I can't imagine what my husband and Stein talk about when they sit around a campfire in the huge darkness.

Once after one of Stein's lectures I dreamed of the disembodied faces of stone angels. Saintly faces from desert frescoes hovered above the bed and in the distance the rock they had been hacked from wept blood like an open wound.

I am fascinated by Ada Lang's strange marriage. I want to know the shape of it, its intimacies and its emptinesses. I want the story behind the fairytale. Because there's always another story.

'There was Shanghai,' says Ken Tiger, 'and there was the French quarter. The French quarter was not China. They even brought their own trees.'

This is the French quarter, with its wide streets and rows of plane trees, its green lawns and tennis courts. It is late afternoon and the streets are empty. Across the gardens comes the sound of a violin.

The Kadoories' house is a white, two-storeyed building with a covered verandah and steps down to a lawn. It was named Marble Hall because of the shiploads of Italian marble imported for the fireplaces. It is a house of scrolls and furbelows, gleaming crystal and stucco. In the ballroom are massive chandeliers. To change a light bulb servants lower the chandeliers with a winch.

To Ada the house's very luxury made it seem insubstantial, a child's fantasy castle. When she tried to explore its depths she found herself facing a window overlooking a street. Marble Hall was designed like a stage set, long and narrow. What was important was the first, sweeping view.

In the mornings the din of the nightsoil cart is the first sound to break the stillness of the dawn. Then the birds and the dogs, the servants moving through the house, winding open the shutters. Already, slowly at first, the house is beginning to stir. Even at this early hour the heat shimmers over the gardens. This is the monsoon season.

Ada sleeps late into the mornings. She lies under swathes of gauzy netting, drowsing in the scented warmth. She sleeps as if by sleeping she can escape the merciless heat of Shanghai. In the first days she had risen with her new husband, slipping on her wrap and eating breakfast with him in their rooms. He would leave her at her dressing table, running a brush idly through her hair. Before he kissed her he would bend down and place his face beside hers, smiling at their twin reflections. The man and his wife.

'What are you going to do with yourself today, my love?' he would ask before he strode off into the morning. Ada would watch at the window as he walked across the lawn to where his black car waited. As soon as the car disappeared down the avenue she would climb back under the mosquito net and drift back into sleep.

A Chinese servant wakes her, a smooth face peering cautiously at her through folds of netting. Does the mistress wish for lunch? Would she like tea brought up? She opens her eyes and stares blankly at the gauzy white world. She had dreamed of snow. Always when she first wakes she forgets. She forgets China, forgets her husband.

The servant brings tea, opens the curtains. The room fills with light and she feels sharp pains behind her eyes. It is one o'clock in the afternoon.

When her husband had come to her on their first night of marriage Ada had thought that perhaps she could lose herself in the warmth of his trembling flesh. As she watched him undress she felt a quiver of arousal and wondered if this was what would take her out of her life. She wanted to believe that this eminently solid *husband* would draw all of her vast self to him. That the landscape of marriage could slide, like a Chinese screen, in front of all her lost worlds. As he moved towards her, his body smooth and pale, she held out her arms, ready to lose herself in the obliterations of desire.

He moved quickly and neatly, folding back the pleats of her nightdress and rising above her, his brow furrowed in concentration. She lay back, feeling the weight of him, closing her eyes and trying to lose herself in the fluid surge and slip. But when he shuddered and collapsed onto her she felt herself as two women, the one stroking her husband's damp black hair, and the other a disembodied spirit who floated somewhere near the ceiling.

After that, whenever he came to her, she felt the watching self, the one who slipped free and hovered beside the bed, gazing dispassionately at her.

Behind the house, where the garbage bins are, beggars squat under the lamppost. They are emaciated, their bellies distended, and half-naked except for pieces of sacking. Some of them are bald from malnutrition. Sometimes there are lepers. These are the beggars of Shanghai. They chatter among themselves, waiting, waiting.

When the kitchen door opens they shove each other to get to the bins, to the food. They tear at the leftovers like animals, slapping and pushing, gorging themselves. When there is nothing left they wander off into the darkness. Some of them stay to sleep under the trees.

Ada can be seen in the distance, walking through the grounds. The servants watch her from the windows of the house. She walks to the edge of the garden, to the street.

There are no cars, the French quarter is drowsing in the void of the siesta. The wide avenues are empty. She doesn't open the gate, only stands looking out at the street.

In the afternoons she lies back in her chair on the wide porch and looks up at the drifting Chinese sky. She feels the boundaries of her world dissolving. In Victor Kadoorie's marble-white house she feels herself hazy and insubstantial. She lies back, watching the oleanders in the sun and thinking of nothing.

Some English women came to see her. Victor Kadoorie had invited them, to cheer her up, he said. They sat on the deck with her, drinking scalding green tea and talking about the heat. One of the women leaned towards her.

'Ada. Now look at me. You mustn't be sad here. Your poor husband worries.'

Ada looked at her. She had a large, pale face and her hair was very light. She had glass earrings that were shaped like drops of water.

'You must try and forget about all the things that have happened to you. You can be happy now. You owe it to your husband.'

The woman put her hand on Ada's arm and smiled at her.

After that, when the women came, Ada spoke to them as if conversation was a trick to be learned. She let them take her to their dressmakers and she learned to pour tea in the afternoons but she never allowed intimacies. To her friends she gave no account of herself. She never spoke of Russia, or of her early life in Shanghai. When her husband held receptions she stood beside him and smiled across the ballroom. She allowed the men to dance with her, always holding herself slightly away from them.

It seemed, they said of her, as if she had an idea of who she was supposed to be, and put up with the idea of that person without ever seeming to be present. Part of her, the women said, always seemed to be evading you, and she had an odd way of half-closing her eyes and retreating into silence.

At Marble Hall Ada insisted that trays of food and jugs of water were put out for the beggars. Sometimes she went out to them and gave out coins. One evening she felt grasping fingers at her skirt and looked down to see a child with one eye gouged out, a raw hole where she should have seen a brown glitter and the curtain of the lid. Her husband came home to find her weeping on the kitchen steps, clutching the filthy child to her. When he tried to prise her fingers away she cried hysterically and demanded that he call a doctor, that something be done. Victor Kadoorie looked down at his wife as if he had never seen her before. He looked at her eyes, dark and wild, and her shaking body and something like horror came into his face. She began to sing to the child, her voice low and crooning, and he turned away and walked inside.

Later he tried to reassure her. 'They do it to their own children, Ada. Cut off a limb or put out an eye. It's purely a ploy for sympathy. It makes them better beggars. You mustn't let it upset you so much.'

Ada said nothing. They had made her wash with kerosene and the clothes she was wearing had been taken away to be burnt.

'If you'd like to do something, some sort of charity work, there are plenty of respectable organisations.'

She looked at her husband. He was standing under a lamp and a circle of yellow light fixed and held him. He stood before her like a saint, pale and illuminated. His cone of light held him forever apart from the sightless world, from suffering, from the darkness.

Ada turned her face away.

Sometimes whole days pass without the sound of another human voice. It's very quiet and still in the university flat. When there are no students around all you can hear is the occasional surge of an engine, the far-off clatter of a drill. There are no trees in the courtyard. In my house in Australia the windows were full of the shapes of the trees. There were fig trees, apricot trees, a Japanese pepper. Outside my bedroom there was a Brazilian jasmine. And beneath the kitchen window a pink camellia that Joseph planted for me.

You shouldn't be alone too much, a friend of mine once told me, it tips you into unreason. I don't know if that's true. Sometimes I go out. I put on a dress and take the train into the city. The city is too full of people. They come at me, the whole surging mass of them, crushing me at the traffic lights, pushing past me on the streets. I walk, I look in the windows of houses, I peer in temple doors, but I don't know how to create any coherency out of these unrelated adventures. And always at the end of the day this high room over the quiet courtyard. A woman drinking tea at a formica table.

Joseph isn't here but there's a photograph of him on the fridge. He looks distant and worn out. His eyes are focused somewhere off to the side, unable to meet mine.

In the afternoons sheets of rain move across the window. The rain here is unlike anywhere else. It's so heavy you can't see your hand in front of your face. Even with a raincoat it pours in warm slicks down the back of the neck.

Sometimes I don't want to see anyone. I'm happy just to lie in bed and watch the rain. Other times the solitude seems untenable. There are excursions in the city I could join. The white women have a kind of weekly adventure club. They hire a van and a Chinese guide and meet in the square. They're easy to spot, there's a fashion among them for pale colours and they're the only ones wearing hats against the sun. The English women carry tan macintoshes. There are a hundred adventures to be had. There are sculptors who carve flowers from jade. There are Chinese operas and oriental gardens. There are shops selling gold and silk. There are local festivals and floating restaurants.

For weeks Clarissa and the other wives have been talking

about the Ching Ming Festival. It's a festival for visiting graves. Headstones are cleaned and food and wine are left for the spirits. In China the dead never stay resolutely dead. They are not like the well-behaved Western dead who are content to lie quietly beneath crumbling stone. The women want to see.

I can understand the impulse. Once, on a cold night, I stood in a graveyard in Mexico. The stones had been painted and they glowed whitely under the soft light of a thousand candles. The dead need a trail of light to find their way home, a woman told me. This was no quiet cemetery of stone and plaster angels. Every grave flamed with flowers and streamers. Children ran between gravestones with sugar candies shaped like skeletons. People sang and drank tequila. Whole families picnicked around dead relatives' graves.

Everywhere there were marigolds. The marigolds are for the *angelitos*, the dead children, my friend told me. They follow the trail of brightness home.

There are no marigolds in the Chinese graveyard. It's a small cemetery, wrapped around the bottom of a green hill near Repulse Bay. Driving along the road to the bay with Clarissa, I have often looked out at the white headstones scattered up and down the slopes. They look like they are tumbling down towards the sea.

The cemetery is full of people. Chinese families, hordes

of them, are milling around in the bleached light. So many shoes and handbags and cigarettes and loud chatter that sounds almost guttural, like a language of the desert. And the sun, the sun of summer, slicing and cutting through it all.

At the graves people are burning incense. The smell of it comes to me, odd and cloying. There are women with their sleeves rolled up, scrubbing gravestones. They look efficient and determined. They could be washing a stubborn pan.

They come to burn paper for the dead, the Chinese guide tells us. There is paper money. There are paper cut-outs of cars and jewels and houses and clothes. Everything you had, or didn't have, in life is burned for you in death.

Clarissa takes my arm. Her dress is gold and she's wearing very red lipstick. She has a bold, handsome sort of face. 'You have to see the shops here,' she says, 'they're hilarious. They buy all this stuff and burn it so their relatives are set up in the next world.'

The paper shops are tucked away in a line behind the cemetery. Inside there are boxes of gold-foil watches, rhinestone jewels, fat wads of fake money written on the Bank of Hell. There are strange dioramas of houses complete with cars in the driveway, servants, mistresses and tiny trays of food. From the ceiling of the shop dangle metre-long papier-mâché servants.

Care moves in strange ways. Even in death we try and protect those we love.

'Need a new cook?' Clarissa spins a dour-faced effigy around. She is walking behind the paper statues and I can see slivers of her between the trembling aprons and paper legs. Behind the counter two women are eating bowls of rice, staring at us without speaking.

In the window are piles of brightly wrapped packages, green and red like Christmas presents, with ribbons and dragon stickers. They are paper clothes. I buy a package. Clarissa laughs. 'You'll be well dressed in the next life.'

Outside we stand and watch the lines of people at the furnace. They clutch handfuls of paper and squint into the sun. A man with a long rod pokes the fluttering paper deep into the fire while people fan the smoke away from their faces.

Clarissa and I buy ice-creams from a man with a cart and sit at a table in the sun. Beyond the cemetery you can see the blue of the sea. We're not close enough to hear its rush and pull.

Clarissa is talking about Joseph. 'They're not popular with the Chinese, you know, your husband and Aurel Stein. Some people aren't too keen about what they do out there in the desert.'

My hands are on the table and my wedding ring catches the sun. Joseph didn't give it to me, this ring. There was no band slipped over the bones of a finger in a hushed church. I didn't want a ring, I had told him. A band of gold didn't have anything to do with love, or with marriage. My mother wore a wedding band for years after her husband disappeared up north. She wore it for years until her fingers grew thin and the metal slipped too easily. A band of gold for a husband who had left her while she was pregnant with her last baby.

It was Gideon who insisted. He was horrified. He didn't think you could be a wife with bare fingers. After the wedding he bought Joseph and I matching gold bands. It seemed silly then not to concede. Joseph lost his in the sea a month later but I kept mine. I became a wife with a gold wedding ring after all.

'But they're working for China,' I say. 'Trying to reconstruct the Chinese past. It's an archaeologist's paradise out there in the desert.'

'Perhaps. But there's a lot of anger about the westerners who've come over the years and carted off Chinese treasures.'

Suddenly the memory of an afternoon at Aurel Stein's house in Australia comes back to me. Left on my own in the lounge room, I had picked up a small pottery bowl, intricately glazed and painted. I was holding it up to the light when I heard Stein's voice behind me.

'That's early Tang. You can see from the design markings. Probably left behind or sold by one of the caravan traders passing through the desert some time in the seventh century. We found it in near Lop Nor.'

'Shouldn't it be in a museum?'

Stein takes the bowl out of my hands and replaces it carefully on the shelf. When he speaks there is a strange note in his voice. 'We've catalogued what we need. Even Mao Zedong said that only samples of the past should be retained.'

'Joseph should watch out,' Clarissa says carefully. She is talking about the Handover. She knows these things from her husband. 'Things might be different soon. I don't care what they do with their antiques and their mummies but the Chinese do. Especially now.'

I look at her. In Hong Kong white women don't talk about politics. 'What are you saying? What are they going to do?'

'I don't know. Anything they want. Who knows? Just tell Joseph to be careful.'

I can't protect my husband. He holds his work to him tightly. Like a secret, like a lover.

Ken Tiger holds an oil lamp above his head, its glare casting a circle in front of us. Three men stare out of the passing darkness. In this world of alleys Hong Kong shrinks to a sprawling hamlet, a maze-world of lanes and courtyards. The road is full of ruts and the light from the lamp dips and bounces as we walk. People emerge like moths from darkened doorways.

We slip into a small courtyard where benches have been set up around a makeshift stage. People move in the darkness and groups gather on the benches, the women holding children on their laps. Some of them speak to Ken Tiger and he raises his hand in greeting.

I had asked him to take me to a shadow play, not the ones

staged for tourists at the big hotels, but the real thing. I liked the idea of a story told with shadows, the narrative bound up in lines of dark and light.

During the play I watch the flickering light from the stage play over his face. I want to know the shape of things, the particular dimensions of his world. I want to cast a lamp on the silk screen of him, uncover the patches of shadow and light.

Afterwards he takes me to a teahouse in a street I've never seen before. Groups of men are clustered around tables, some of them are playing dominoes. Ken Tiger orders tea and sweet lotus cakes. The cakes are a concession to me. They are moist and sticky. I can't manage more than a few mouthfuls.

Ken Tiger is watching the slide of the tiles on the table next to us. I want him to talk about himself, about the shape of those early years. I imagine I might be able to see her in his memories, that in the inflections of his voice I might hear hers.

But it's the master he wants to talk about, not the woman. He wants to tell me about Du Yue-sheng.

'In those years I loved Du more than I had loved anyone in my life. We all did. We had nothing, we were country boys with no shoes and he made us think that Shanghai was ours. And we believed him. We would have done anything for him. And we did.'

He's talking about him as if he was a legend, a hero, a

kind of Chinese Fagin. I looked up Du. You can spend hours scanning microforms, flicking through old news stories and you still have little more than a line of facts. A pad full of jotted notes and a photocopied face, dark and indistinct.

In the stories Du Yue-sheng is larger than life, a man with a monkey's head at his back and an army of boys at his feet. His name is linked to every kind of skulduggery imaginable. The papers are full of stories of opium smuggling and song-girls. Intrigues abound, dastardly murders, shady deals. He was clever and in Shanghai he had a hand in everything.

For the boys he enlists there are rolled mats on the floor, a fire in winter and food in the evenings. The new boys sometimes cry in the night, the noise muffled in their shirts. They are fresh from the country, fresh from their mothers and they don't know the ways of the city.

They soon learn. It begins with a hand in a coat pocket, the slip of a wallet from a jacket. For the clever ones there are more lessons, bigger prizes. They put aside their tear-streaked memories of village harvests and learn to trade in crime. When they do well Du gives them money, sticky cakes of opium, women.

Early on Du took a liking to the boy from Pudong. He gave him a slim knife and a new suit and sent him on special errands. The boy was clever, he picked up English quickly and he was loyal. Du made him his special attendant. For him the spoils of the kill, the golden ducks and shining trout of Du's table, the warmth of a wool coat in winter, the clatter of gold pieces.

In those first years the young man did everything asked of him with a kind of filial devotion. He was quick and unflinching, he could move invisibly in the shadows. Du had given him a home and a future and wealth he could never have dreamed of in his village boyhood. He admired Du's single-mindedness, his self-enclosure. At night he wrote poetry in his room. He is young and eager, he cannot resist the temptations of sentimentality. He feels himself a huge vessel, everything he sees he wants to absorb, to understand, to tell. I can see him, his long-ago face in a circle of light, his hand sliding over the page before him.

As Du grew older his superstitions became almost a madness. He consulted soothsayers and fortune tellers, called in geomancers and palm readers. He became gripped by images of his own death and sent his young attendant out in search of exotic and bizarre curatives to prolong life.

'Perhaps,' says Ken Tiger, 'it was the thought of so much blood on his hands that made him so afraid. I'd like to think so.'

He is quiet for a long time. Looking at him I think that we can never really tell our own histories. How can we summon up the specific images we need, the particular images, the inflections of voice and the hot weight of tears?

'He was convinced that everyone was trying to murder him. He became paranoid. There had to be four guards at his bed. He had someone test all his food before he ate. He was mad.'

I know from the newspaper articles that Du wasn't murdered. There was no knife in the back, no poisoned wine. His death, when it came, was quiet and uneventful. His favourite attendant was there to lower the sheet over his face.

'By that time I had enough money to go into business for myself,' says Ken Tiger. 'I bought one of the stone houses in the Chinese quarter. I didn't want to live with the French. I had a house, a business, some money. Then I met Ada Kadoorie.'

'Tell me about Ada,' I say to Ken Tiger. 'Tell me about the first time you saw her.'

The old man closes his eyes. 'Did you ever,' he says slowly, 'feel your life changed forever by a single moment?'

I think of a room full of sun, of light blazing through windows, of a face suspended in liquid light. A face illuminated. *Yes.*

'When I think of that first day …' He stops and I see that his hands are trembling. His eyes are shining. I like a man who isn't afraid of tears. A man who believes that the past is not always intact, that a single moment will wait for you like the card table waits for the gambler.

'It's her hair I think of,' he says. 'Her face looking up at me through her hair. I wanted to touch it. It looked like the sun.'

The evening is bright and clear. I settle into my chair and pull my cardigan around my shoulders. Sometimes at night there is a faint chill in the air. This gently seeping chill is the only way that you can tell that it is winter in the city. Maybe it's different in the villages or up-country, I don't know. It's never cold enough for wool against the skin.

The lovers' meeting is story-like, spectacular. Fate intervenes to bring them together. Arms encircle a waist, the woman is pulled from sudden danger. A slack thread tightens and they feel themselves walking the taut line of a tightrope.

In winter the afternoons are dark. Ada lies safe beneath the white gauze. She is very still. She hears light footsteps in the hall and the maid pushes the door open and peers at Ada through the filmy cloth. 'Snow!' she says, 'I thought you like to see.'

Ada stares at her. She climbs out of bed and walks into the cold hall and they stand together at the big window. Before the window the flakes float and drift, fine slivers of spun ice. Below them the lawn is white and glistening and the street shines under the soft light of the lamps. Snow lies on the road, the plane trees, the high stone of the houses. The light is fine and shadowless, it is the light of her dreams.

Under snow the city seems even less substantial. People

and places lose their solidity. She sees her husband coming across the lawn, an airy shape wrapped in crushed ice. She watches snowflakes touch the glass of the window and turn to streams of melting ice. In the winter of Shanghai she feels herself adrift, floating.

In the snow Ada takes up walking again. It is too cold to sit on the porch and the marble house has become a kind of prison.

She stands outside the gate, looking down the avenue to where it curves away into shadows. The road is white with new snow. In the long months of summer she could never have imagined that snow came to this place. She pulls the thick coat her husband has given her close around her. It is lined with soft fur. She is not a woman who minds the feel of an animal's pelt against the skin. In the country she comes from flesh is always enclosed in fur. The women adorn themselves in the skins of bears, seals, and wolves.

She pushes through all the new squares of fresh snow. She passes plane trees thin and white with the breath of frost. Ahead of her a horse slips on the smooth ice of the road. She watches the carriage lurch to one side and then tip back onto the road, disaster narrowly avoided.

Ada Kadoorie has become a familiar figure. She walks the wide streets of the French quarter, her head bare, her hair shining in the winter sun. Sometimes she traces the road along the river, stepping quickly between carriages and rickshaws, and stops to look at the harbour. Gazing down at the lines of ships she sees the world made transversable, escape a possibility.

Years before in Russia there was a story of a woman who, after sailing away to the New World, became stricken with longing for her own land. She sat in her American husband's house, looking out at wheatfields and weeping for snow. Her husband wanted help with the milking and a bowl of porridge in the mornings. He didn't say much to her. Sometimes telegraphs came from Russia. Her mother sent one if there was a birth or a death. The woman walked the seven miles to the post office to decipher her mother's joy or despair. She liked the idea of telegraph lines stretching neatly across the globe, from the wheatfield town to her own city. She thought that if she followed the telegraph lines she could surely find her way home. One day she took some money from a tin box and some food from the pantry, left her husband in the wheatfield and set out along the telegraph wires. She didn't think about bodies of water or lines under oceans. She was convinced, this Russian woman, that the world was not unfathomable, that if a line of words could travel halfway around the globe then so could she.

She became a legend. According to the story she appeared, almost a year later, in Siberia. She was half-starved and blue with cold. She gave no account of her journey, saying only that she had come as telegraphs come.

In Shanghai, Ada thinks of telegraph lines stretching from one world to another. She thinks about exile and the possibilities of return. She knows that a woman walked home from America, that Napoleon returned triumphant from a rock in the sea. Then she thinks of the boots of soldiers and blood, like bright rubies, sprinkled on the snow.

She walks along the Bund, past the Grecian columns of the Hongkong and Shanghai Bank. It is all white scrolls and curving steps. The entrance is flanked by a pair of golden lions, one in a roaring posture, the other in repose. Every day, hundreds of Chinese stop to rub the nose and paws of the lions. *They're a superstitious race, her husband has told her, they think it will improve their joss. That some of the luck of the British might rub off.* Ada has seen countless hands stretched up to the lions. The hands of coolies and rickshaw boys, silk-suited businessmen and small children. She stops and places her hand on the nose of the recumbent lion. The gold has been rubbed so many times that the bronze beneath shows dully through.

She likes to walk through the neighbourhoods beyond the Bund. The Chinese part of the city. She wants the tiny worlds that exist behind the exterior of the city. In all her wanderings the streets never become familiar. The alleys dissolve and remake themselves daily, street signs change, landmarks disappear. Shanghai is a city built on water and its neighbourhoods are slippery and changeable.

In some alleys the balconies of the houses above close in

like an arch above her head. The false twilight is illuminated by paraffin lamps and light bulbs strung over the stalls. An old woman squats in a doorway cutting pieces of sugar cane. A calligrapher works at his streetside stall, red banners full of gold characters hanging all around him. Hawkers trail handcarts through the mud of the streets. Men stumble, corpse-like, from the doorways of opium houses, the sweet smell of smoke circling up onto the street. The streets are all motion and clamour, all around her people ripple, sombre faces loom out of dark corners. She stares at the faces around her, watching dark eyes slide away from hers. She passes houses ransacked in the fighting with the Japanese. Shutters hang from their gaping windows and sometimes she catches sight of shadowy figures in their burnt-out interiors.

Midwinter is a festival of light. On the fifteenth night of the first moon they light lanterns and burn them through the night. On the river a procession of paper boxes alive with flame stretches as far as the eye can see. Every house is ablaze with lanterns.

Ada has asked her husband to tell her the story of this festival of lanterns. They are having lunch, the table smooth and wide between them, a servant hovering in the shadows. These lunches are all the same. He smiles and looks at his wife, her face eager, her hair glowing in the soft light. Her elbows are resting on the table like a child's. These are the simple stories, the ones he can explain across the table.

'Long ago,' he begins, 'the Jade Emperor became so angry with a village for killing his favourite goose, he decided to destroy it with a storm of fire. Some spirit heard his plan and came and warned the villagers to light lanterns. They did so and from above it looked like the village was ablaze. It was a clever trick. When he looked down the Jade Emperor was satisfied that the village was already burning so he didn't destroy them. So every year they light lanterns to celebrate their deliverance.'

'How wonderful!' Ada is delighted.

'It's a nice fairytale, isn't it?'

'But Victor,' she looks up at her husband, 'we have miracles of light too! Hanukkah!'

'It's hardly the same as a pagan myth, Ada.'

'But it's the same story. Deliverance from destruction, the miracle of the temple lamps, lighting candles every year to celebrate. It's the same!'

Victor Kadoorie stares at his wife. She is watching him, her chin in her hands, her eyes bright. He pushes back his chair and walks from the room.

Ada watches her husband's disappearing back. She is thinking of a world where vengeful gods send floods and plagues, where angels come to warn and to announce and where lamb's blood on the door can save you from destruction.

In the afternoon, after the siesta, the same winter coat, the same buttoned boots and away she goes. Into the street, through the French quarter to the Chinese city.

It's the first time in days she has been able to get away. The Chinese New Year brings rounds of celebrations, parties and visiting. Her husband in his fine silk suit had handed out little red envelopes of money to the servants, watching each smooth head bow before him. The whole house had been filled with peonies. A lucky flower, her maid had told her, her arms full of the heavy blooms. Ada watched the woman carefully arranging the flowers on her dressing table, biting on her lip in concentration as she moved the stems.

'Take some for yourself,' Ada had said, 'I don't need so many. Take some for your room.'

Her husband had given her a dress of red silk. The whole room had blazed scarlet when she stood in front of the mirror. She liked the way the silk fell against the skin. Smooth and fluid, leaving a cool space between the cloth and the flesh.

Later they stood and watched the sky light up with fireworks. The sky of the dry season is very high and clear and the colours flame spectacularly against it. Victor Kadoorie watched his wife's transfixed face, the fireworks casting lurid shadows on her skin.

In the Chinese city, the poor have their own observations. In the cold darkness of the alleyways they stop the flow of time to commemorate gods and events. Lanterns burn in every window and the thin screen of reality is suspended. In front of one of the shops they are roasting a slab of meat on a spit, the flesh sizzling as it turns. In the streets barefooted children let off fireworks.

Ada wanders through the streets, her face turned to the lights, her feet feeling their way on the damp flagstones.

What happens is too fast to remember clearly. From an unseen corner a horse, broken free of its tethers, lurches into the street. Gunpowder explodes, colours dazzle and the beast rears up and charges. Ada, her head turned, feels the hot weight of flesh, the wild brown neck, the heaviness and the force of the lunging flanks.

As she falls back onto the pavement she sees the horse's terrified eyes, its lips stretched wide. She falls heavily. Her hands feel the wetness of stone and her head strikes the edge of a door. The lights flicker and she closes her eyes.

The young man standing in the doorway acts quickly. Strong arms encircle her, hands spread around her waist. She feels the firmness of flesh, leans back into an easy embrace. Hearts beat, time stops. The noise is deafening, the surge of the crowd dangerous. She feels herself pulled backwards into the stillness of an inner space, hears a door closed against the street.

Her rescuer lowers her gently onto a wicker lounge. His hands linger for a second on her waist and when they are gone she feels the imprint of his fingers against her skin. She looks up dizzily.

How difficult, to evoke a lost face. To remember lines, as fine then as India ink, which have loosened and flowed away. The face is smooth, golden against the dimness of the room. The eyes float towards her, the dark pupils, the fine lids, the curtain of lashes all exactly delineated. She wants to reach up and touch him.

The story begins long before this vision of the face. It is only the first image, new and therefore detached from all the rest. The story begins long ago, in Ada Lang's desire for something to seize her out of herself, in the young man's longing for something to reveal his own soul to him.

They will meet again the next day.

And again the day after.

When he puts his hands against her skin the room flares dizzily around her. She wants to wrap her body around his like a blazing streak of light, to be burned up in him. There is a tremor which begins on the surface of the skin and spreads all the way to the pit of the belly. *It is like a pleasant kind of seasickness,* she thinks to herself as he unbuttons his shirt. The chest is fine and slender. Her hands mark every ridge of bone, every curve of vertebrae. So narrow, the ribs, and yet strong.

When he slides his hand under her shift she feels that the shape of her body is being drawn for the first time. That he has taken a brush and painted the lines and the curves of her. The flesh pours into this new body. Its very corporeality astonishes her. Shopping for silk, walking the streets, she feels his hands on her skin, the hot brand of his breath on her neck. Lying awake in bed, her husband's sleeping form curled away from her in the darkness, she wonders what she will do with this excess of desire. She sees the face of her lover, shimmering on the speckled moonlight ceiling, and her whole body arches with longing. This is what she had wanted, yes, this.

The first days of spring. It's here in the streets of Shanghai, in the avenues of the French Concession, in the room where the lovers lie. Soon the rains will come and the whole city will drown in the heat, but for now the days are mild and long. Outside, the noises of the street, the click of wheels, hawkers' cries, the wail of a radio. Ada lies with her head against his chest. How clever the body, the always-pumping heart so neatly held by the ribs, so safe behind filigrees of bone.

Her words occupy everything. She tells him stories, spinning them into an endless skein for his skin, smooth as silk. She talks of a world of silence, a wilderness of white. Snow, she says, like diamonds, so bright the eyes begin to water. The winter of Shanghai is nothing, she tells him, compared to the cold of her country. There the cold seeps through every bone and the snow is savage, it hurls itself at you like stones. But such beauty, she tells him. The frozen pink haze of dawn, the contours of her village shimmering under the weight of snow. The world remade white and perfect. The berries that live under the ice, staining her hands crimson in summer. The red embers of the fire, the trails through the forest, rich women who decorate themselves with the skins of silver foxes.

'Where I come from,' says Ada, 'trees fall under the weight of snow. They're lost in the snow. Sometimes whole villages are lost. It can take days to dig them out.'

He wants to tell her his stories, wants to offer up great tracts of his life for her but he doesn't have the words to weave a narrative. Her English is still faltering, sometimes when he speaks to her he feels her dissolving and disappearing. The past drifts into the room and he feels unequal to it. All he has are images. His mother standing by the edge of a still lake, her hands full of mangoes, the thin lines of smoke above the rooftops, a green slipper sleeping beneath the sand.

He shows her a photograph. A family group posed stiffly in front of a painted landscape. A father in a woollen cap, four sisters, a mother with bewildered eyes, hands crossed in her lap. And him. The son, the treasured thing, the handsome face, the hand resting on the mother's shoulder.

'You are their treasure,' she whispers, liking the way the English word pushes like a breath on the tongue. *Treasure*.

'Your treasure,' he says, kissing her. 'Yours.'

But this is a woman who has lost her country, her family, her people. She has none of the anxieties of possession.

The days have a clarity to them. They hang suspended like crystal prisms across a window and the discs of light they scatter are the colour of her hair. There is a smell of incense and the faint shapes of small geckoes flicker on the walls. Bamboo blinds filter the sunlight.

When we first came I asked Joseph to show me his China.

Somewhere, past Lantau Island and Macao, where the horizon blends into a blurry land mass, is China. I have never been. China is a place where Hong Kong people never go. China is a place you leave. You leave the desperate muddy villages, the teeming cities, the broken things. You leave houses, spare and dusty rooms, box apartments, clocks that never tell the right time. You leave mothers and brothers and sisters and sometimes, children. And you come. By fishing boat in the dark with the fisherman's cracked brown hand pressing into your thigh, or by treachery or by money.

'China is shit,' says Mei, the Chinese woman employed by the university to clean our apartment once a week. It's crazy, really, that they send her. I could take care of the place myself. Run a vacuum over the tatty rug, wash the lino, wipe the dust off the window ledge. There's not much to do.

Still she comes, every Tuesday morning, unsmiling in her beige overalls, clanging the buckets and brushes in a slightly resentful way.

'You no go China, miss,' she says, banging a pile of dishes into the sink. 'It's shit. Nothing there.'

'Will you ever go back?'

She looks at me like I am crazy. 'What for I go back? For no food, for no job?'

I look down at my hands. Mei is probably an *eye-eye*, an illegal immigrant, Joseph says. She came from Zhongshan, the same village as Sun Yat-sen. The lychees we eat come from Zhongshan. Lychees and Sun Yat-sen. I'm sure that's not what Mei thinks of when she thinks of her home.

I try another tack. 'What is the feeling in China about Mao Zedong now?' Joseph has told me that it is only now that people are beginning to come to terms with the horror of the Cultural Revolution, to speak about it.

Mei stares at me coldly for a moment and turns back to the dishes. Her small shoulders jerk up and down as she scrubs a plate.

Sometimes I feel as if I live in a country of people I'll never comprehend. People of fine poetry and exquisite paintings, who could be so blindly led. Who, for a decade of peculiar horror, became the instruments of their own torture. I read in a book on Mao that in one province alone, more than seventy-five different methods of torture were invented.

There is another China. Another place apart from the one people leave, from the one that has been scourged by war and plunder, mass murder, chaos, upheaval. It is exotic and it is much further away than the China you can get to in under an hour on the main line from Kowloon Tong. It is fragrant teas and delicate glazed cups proffered to me as if to compensate for all the time it claims. It is Joseph's China and I know nothing of it.

Hong Kong is not China. The words might be changing — colony, territory — but it is all the same really. It seems strange to me, the idea of borrowing a place. Borrowing it and then giving it back.

Clarissa says that they've known about the Handover since 1984. 'We're all sick of the bloody Handover before it's even happened,' she laughs. 'It's always Handover this, Handover that, all the radio stations are full of it, the newspapers, the dailies. Hire a hotel room for the big night. It'll be like New Year's. Sneak up on you and happen and that's that.'

The way she says it reminds me of the story of the opening of the Sydney Harbour Bridge. The stolen opening.

The official party and the governor with his silver scissors and the long silk ribbon stretched between the steel pillars and then the rebel, the daring rabble-rouser galloping through on a horse and slicing the ribbon while the stunned crowd and the furious governor gape. It happened and that was that.

I asked Joseph to show me his China. I have read about a temple of ten thousand Buddhas, about a mummified body embalmed in gold leaf. I wanted to look at China through the lens of his sight, to see if I could love it too.

'I'll see,' he said. The next night he came home with tickets for a concert. The Vienna Boys' Choir, at the Convention Centre by the harbour.

'Come on Maya,' he says, smiling the old smile at me. 'It's no Chinese opera, I know, but there's nothing wrong with a bit of western nostalgia.'

He's strangely light-hearted. On the street a bike careens towards us and he takes my arm loosely, pulling me back from the road. I love him, and sometimes I think he loves me.

All those small boys in sailor suits, singing like angels, holding the notes so high and long. I wonder what kind of life it is for them, singing on stages all over the world, raising their voices to the gods of a hundred different countries. Little lost boys sleeping bunk to bunk in dormitories in Vienna. Standing on their steps for long hours while choir masters recite new Latin words to learn. And back in the villages the voices of the brothers and the sisters raised only in laughter and play.

In the darkness of the concert hall I watch Joseph's face. He rests his chin on his hand and half-closes his eyes. I would like to lead him back to our bed by the window overlooking the sea, to fall asleep with his hand clasped between my breasts, his breath against my neck.

In our first years together we would sometimes lie in bed in the early evenings while the light changed and the crickets started. From the bedroom window we watched the falling dark, drinking cold gin from tumblers, talking a little and pulling up the sheets when the breeze came in off the ocean. Joseph would bring a plate of olives and cheese from the kitchen, a slab of bread, and we would eat in bed, listening to the sound of the waves.

Those nights have a kind of inviolable quality to them now. Sometimes I think that if only we could lie on that bed again from dusk until early morning, we might be safe.

In Hong Kong the newspapers are full of violence. Kidnappings, disappearances, business rivalries turned ugly. Today there is a story of a woman disfigured by acid thrown at her face by the jealous mistress of her banker husband. It's not the first story of its kind I've heard here.

I stand at the window of the apartment. On the stones of the courtyard there's a stain that looks like a body. The spreading water takes the shape of arms, feet, a head. It is late, there is dust on the windowsill and a dying moth is flapping its papery wings. You can't touch moths, my mother used to tell us, there's a special dust on their wing that makes them fly. If you touch them you rub it off and they're grounded, helpless. Joseph laughed when I told him that story. 'My fanciful wife,' he said. 'Sometimes I think there's no end to your gullibility.' He explained that it isn't magic dust that makes moths fly, it's the minute structures on the wings, the tiny hairs and scales designed for flight.

Joseph sits in my chair by the window of the apartment. His face is lean and tanned from the desert. He sits in silence, staring out the dusty window. If only I could walk the six paces across the room and touch him perhaps we would be safe.

There is trouble for Joseph and Aurel Stein. The Chinese want the mummy they call the Beauty of Loulan back. They are claiming that it was stolen from them and demanding an end to all unauthorised exploration in the Taklamakan. They no longer want artefacts that are part of their national heritage removed to western museums.

'Fucking hypocrites,' Joseph says. His jaw is tight with rage.

He is so angry because there has been, until now, little interest from the Chinese in excavating their own history. Only a silence in the face of antiquity. Their conception of the past is too fluid and changeable to allow them to go in for the kind of cataloguing and recording that obsesses Joseph. And in the new China, eyes are always on the future, not the dusty relics of some half-remembered past.

But this sudden interest is not historical. The Beauty of Loulan is dangerous for the Chinese. They have seen the pictures of her famous red hair and fine features splashed briefly across the pages of newspapers, heard the less publicised conjectures that this discovery could change received history about the Tarim Basin. Somewhere in their bureaus of information is Joseph and Aurel Stein's monograph describing their theory that Europeans were first in the desert, not the Chinese.

'Why does it matter so much?'

'Bloody hell, Maya, I've been through this.' Joseph pushes his hair back angrily. 'It matters because that whole area is being brutally fought over. The Uighurs want an autonomous territory. The Chinese want the resources. So they're systematically terrorising the Uighurs. Disappearances, bodies, villages burned. If we prove that the Chinese weren't there first, their claim over the area goes out the window!' A vein is pulsing at the side of his head.

'But why is it so important to you?'

Joseph slams his fist on the table. 'For God's sake, Maya.' He storms out of the apartment. I can hear his angry footsteps along the hall.

I've seen this rage in him before.

On our last afternoon in Perth we went to say goodbye to his father. Gideon moved a table out under the jacaranda tree and laid out a slab of cheese, bread, bottles of cold beer. Joseph took his place at the table opposite his father. He hadn't wanted to come.

It's all there. The ragged edge of the lawn, the house with all the windows open for the heat, the hazy light falling through the jacaranda leaves. None of the plates match and there's only one knife for the bread and the cheese. For as long as I've known Gideon he's lived in his house like he was camping out in it. Chipped enamel dishes and pickle jars full of sugar, tea and coffee are lined up on a trestle table. There's one old armchair in the main room and some toolboxes lined up neatly in front of the fireplace. No pictures on the walls, just a calendar with a photograph of some snow-capped mountains that's hung on the back of a door for years. Someone's stuck drawing-pins into the corners to stop the yellowing edges from curling in. I don't know what happened to all their things, to Hannah's furniture, the embroidered sheets and table runners she brought in a steamer trunk from Melbourne.

On our last day in Australia Gideon sat on an upturned milk crate and raised his beer to his son across the table.

'To China. Hope it treats you well.' For a moment the sunlight fell directly on his face and I was struck by how old he looked. An old man. As he turned to me he bumped the flimsy table and a glass of beer tipped over and poured straight into Joseph's lap.

'Jesus Christ!' Joseph jumped to his feet, holding the dripping fabric of his trousers away from his skin. 'How am I supposed to catch a fucking plane like this?' He stalked away into the house and Gideon looked downcast. He shrugged his shoulders, palms held out in silent apology to his son. I watched him looking miserably down at his lap as

Joseph came back to the table, tight-lipped and angry.

For so long I had wanted to be the string between them. The feminine force that brought them together. Over dinners, over glasses of wine, later perhaps over a baby whose small face they could pick out their shared features in.

As we left, Gideon clapped a hand awkwardly on his son's shoulder. 'Look after her,' he said as we walked towards the car.

The grief of love in that tired face, those sloping shoulders, I cannot forget.

For a long time I feel like I have been breaking myself against the wall of my husband, this almost cruel pride he takes in his own self-enclosure. In the beginning I thought of it as a challenge, something I had to break through to get to the real heart of him, to unlock the thing in him that would adore me, love me with a kind of intensity all the more ravishing for its elusiveness. And there were moments. Oh yes, there were moments.

Once he made love to me in a garden. It was in another city, in a botanical garden by a cathedral. I wore a white dress, slipped my cool hand against his neck. I could always use desire to draw him to me then. He seized my wrist and led me further into the garden, into the damp heavy cover of trees. Then he sank to his knees before me, his face hot against the gauzy material of my dress, his hands moving hungrily over my body. I remember the salty taste of his fingers then, the paleness of his skin in the moonlight coming through the trees.

Joseph has never wanted me to be beholden to him. I must always remember to impersonate the woman in those night time gardens, with her white dress and allure. I have only to be the woman who captivated him, the author, the successful academic with her quick clever face and proud reserve. The woman with her own life, her own passions, her own elusiveness.

But something in me falters and I see the unspoken exasperation in his face.

*T*he long Hong Kong evenings, the hot whiff of the river, the lights burning on the sampans in the harbour.

Aurel Stein stands looking out over the water, a good cigar in his hand. It is one of the indulgences he allows himself, these night walks, the sweet heady draw of tobacco. Music drifts across the water from one of the junks moored further out. He can make out the strains of a saxophone and the accompanying chords of a piano. His dog stays close to his heels, quiet and obedient.

The man squatting behind him in the darkness of the empty fish stalls is smoking too, his eyes never leaving Stein's dark silhouette. It is a hot evening and the smells of the river and the fish stalls rise thickly in the air. The man flicks his cigarette *away and rests his elbows on his thighs. He is wearing cheap sandals and a t-shirt emblazoned with an American flag.*

A motorised junk passes close to the jetty, casting a muddy light over the empty docks. The man waits until the boat has passed and then moves quickly to where Stein is standing. In the darkness he slides a knife swiftly in the place beneath the left shoulder blade, where the heart is. Stein staggers backwards, into the man's arms, his body falling heavily. The man hooks his arms under Stein's shoulders, feeling the body jerk and the blood pooling thick and warm against his chest. He heaves Stein towards the edge of the jetty and pushes him over, stepping swiftly backwards as the body lurches into the water. Then he wipes his hands on the back of his pants and walks away along the dock.

In the darkness Stein's body slips silently below the water.

In autumn Ken Tiger brings Ada mooncakes. They are sweet and damp, full of dates and ground lotus. Some contain a whole duck egg, perfectly held in moist sweetness.

'Mooncakes,' he tells her, 'are from the fourteenth century. The plans for an uprising against the Mongols were passed around in cakes.'

Ada is sitting cross-legged on the bed, her hair damp and curling against her neck, a mooncake in her hands. Sometimes he watches this woman and sees the nebulous flare of her memories, her dreams. A whole self held far away and unreachable.

'You must teach me how to make them. So that when I

go home to Russia I can send messages in mooncakes.'

Later he lies watching her as she sleeps, her bright hair falling across her face, a hand flung across the bed. He nestles into the warm curves of her, hears the soft rush of her breath. His face inches from hers, he wants to whisper *don't go, don't ever leave. Stay with me,* but the words are too grave and they slip beneath the surface.

It's in the summer that Ada Lang starts to withdraw from Ken Tiger's world. When she starts to move beyond the place where encircling arms can save you. It's after she first speaks the words *when I go home* that the shape of things begins to change and love begins to shift.

In the dimness of the room he watches his lover dress. She pulls a shift over her skinny frame, a blue dress. Her hair is hanging long and wild, it reaches down to the middle of her back now. He realises that he has linked his life, his fate, to this woman.

Every day he tries to talk to her about the future. Come away, he says. He wants her to leave the marble house, leave the other worlds she inhabits. He wants to take her away.

She leans over him and traces the fine smooth skin of his stomach. This is a woman who knows that things can change in a day. There's something in her that's beyond the power of anyone's grasp. Her husband recognised this soon after he married her and in the slow months of summer her lover begins to see something unsafe and faraway about her.

The week before he had admired the tiny diamonds flashing at her ears. 'I ask my husband to buy me jewellery,' she had said, 'because I know I'll need it later.'

Later. It's a hard word for a lover.

I don't know how to tell the things Ada Lang never said. I don't know what it meant to her, the hours in that room. Did she go to him because in his arms she could lose herself for a little while? Because he helped with her forgetting? Was it only her desire to forget or was it something more?

These are the things he knows about her:

Her voice. It is as you would imagine, soft and low. Sometimes when she speaks it's as if she's absent. She's removed herself from the words and she's lost somewhere between memory and forgetting. Sometimes she scarcely speaks, other times she chatters to him endlessly. When he asks about her family she turns away. She refuses all his questions, begins to sing a tuneless song in another language. He can't bear the voice she has then and he has to leave the room, leave her.

Her face. Sometimes it's the face he knows. The white skin, luminous. The eyes, dark and wide. And sometimes it's another face. He watches her leave him, forget the room, Shanghai, herself.

Sometimes she wakes up confused. She asks him where she is. She looks around the room as if she doesn't know it, as if she's never been there before. As if she's spent so long caught between the new world and the old one that she's forgotten which is which.

Ada lies in the bed by the window, resting her head on her arm, her body still damp from lovemaking. Along her arm is a line of bruises where he has grasped her too firmly. Her lover wants to claim her but she wants only a dissolving into sensation. She wants propinquity without possession.

He doesn't know what her silences mean. The hard, absent look in her eyes. The shape of her spine curving away from him. And the long wordless spaces between them.

There are stories she hasn't told him. He doesn't know that she carries inside her the memory of swollen faces and steel-capped boots. The memory of a spreading pool of redness against the white of snow. Of the hard ring of steel against the spine. Of the terrible things done to women under the trees of the forest.

They were the things that love couldn't get at.

Victor Kadoorie worries about madness. Sometimes in the night he hears his wife call out in her own language. Once he saw her half-awake, shaking at the French doors.

Perhaps madness ran in her family, he doesn't know anything about them. He doesn't know very much about his wife at all, he thinks, a frown coming between his handsome brows. But there's no time to think about that now.

Shanghai is in turmoil. The communists are coming, there's talk of it from the north. A city like Shanghai, built on money and chance, will never be allowed to survive. It was a brief spring, the rise of this city, and he knows he has to get out. All around him people are packing up and leaving. The war is over and the exiled Jews have shipped out in boatloads bound for America, for Australia. Victor Kadoorie is thinking of Hong Kong.

Ada still goes every day to the house in the Chinese quarter but her lover is different. Sometimes he closes his eyes and she sees his lips quivering. He's full of images of her leaving, his abandonment. Every time she slips her dress on and walks out of the room he imagines that it is the last time. That later has arrived.

Again and again he speaks to her of escape, of safe ships on flashing seas, of America. Every day she says that she can't come away with him, she's going home.

One day he puts his head down on the table and weeps. Perhaps it's a good thing, he says, that her husband is taking her away on a ship to Hong Kong. Because then she won't be able to give him any more pain. Ada leans over and takes his face between her hands. 'Not Hong Kong,' she says, 'Russia.'

The lovers are lying together by the open window, the rain a cool shock after the heat of the day. The young man stretches his hand out to feel the rain against his skin.

'I don't believe you want me as anything more than your secret lover,' he says. Ada is silent. 'Do you want a life with me, Ada?'

'I don't know,' she whispers, very near to him.

Ken Tiger turns to me and I can see one tear on his cheek. Just a single tear. 'I don't know what our relationship was,' he says. 'A kind of escapism, a fantasy? Who knows these things?'

He stands up and walks to the window, looking out at the street. 'She went back to her husband. I demanded too much from her. I thought there could be a happy ending.'

The room has darkened and outside the brief downpour fills the streets. By morning it will have been dried up by the hot air. Shouts from the laneways drift into the room. Ada sits on the edge of the bed, hugging her arms around her knees, enclosed within herself.

'Don't ever come here again. Do you understand?' he says to her. He sees her wince, the look of pain on her face.

'Yes.'

'What happened then?' I watch the stillness in his face as he speaks. Sometimes I think he has forgotten that I am there.

'I think I went mad during those last days in Shanghai. The communists were just around the corner. Victor Kadoorie was getting ready to move his whole business to Hong Kong. All I could think about was her. I became convinced that she had found another lover. That everything she had said to me was a lie. Once I saw her on the street talking to another man, some business associate of Victor's, and I had the man followed for a week just to see if there was anything between them.'

I stare at Ken Tiger. Still I cannot reconcile this elegant old man with someone who had people followed. A gangster. A criminal.

Of this part of his life he discloses very little. He is not trying to withhold things from me, he says, but I must understand that that part of his life is over now. Now he is just a simple bookseller. An old man.

I know that before he met Ada, Du Yue-sheng allowed him to go into business on his own. I don't know what kind of business, but he told me that he was never as successful as Du because he didn't have the same stomach for it. He set up his offices and bought a house in the Chinese quarter but he was restless and lonely. He spent hours reading. First the Chinese poets and then English writers, Russians, French. He dreamed of his mother and his sisters and the snows of his village. And then he met Ada.

In Hong Kong, when it was all over, he didn't have the heart to continue with the business so he appointed a manager and returned to his books.

In the evenings at Marble Hall, Ada draws a chair close to

the fire and reads, cutting the pages with a knife she grips firmly in her small hand. Victor watches her from across the room, her mouth slightly open, bending into the book as if hypnotised. He watches her wide mouth making shapes around the words, her fine skin, her long hair. Her beauty is just as sharp as the day he first laid eyes on her, but he is beginning to see in her something large and confusing, a private nature that he knows he will never be able to come close to.

He has heard whispers of her affair with a Chinese man but he has refused to believe them. Tonight, staring at his wife's face, he wonders what she might be capable of. Here is a heart that was beyond him.

Clarissa calls me early one morning. 'Let's go to Macao. Yes, now. You've never been. We'll go to the casinos and get sloshed.'

She has an air of excitement about her, and a happy, ringing voice. She eats her food with relish. I've seen her on a shopping tour of the markets point to a yellow row of preserved meat and call out loudly, 'Pigs' dicks! That's what they are!' She crowed about it for days afterwards. 'All those respectable women standing in front of a row of pigs' dicks!'

I can see her now, standing in her cool high-ceilinged house twisting the phone cord in her hands. The colony is full of women like her. Trailing wives. Lost to history, pale from too much time avoiding the sun, they know how to order a six-course meal and where to shop for pearls and jade.

So we go to Macao, sitting in the sun on the creaking Star Ferry and in the air-conditioned chill of the jetfoil. Through the portholes faint grey shapes flash by, rising dimly out of the hazy horizon.

'Lantau Island,' says Clarissa, pointing to one. And later, 'China.'

I stare out at Macao as the boat pulls up to the pier. There are casinos and gleaming white hotels dotted up and down the cliffs. At the water's edge I can see people on the terraces of the hotels, eating, laughing, looking out at the harbour. Everything seems still and sleepy in the midday sun.

The cab takes us up winding roads, past gardens and old villas. Some of the roads are paved with cobblestones and the light is different here, it is the light of Europe.

'It reminds me of Lisbon,' says Clarissa. 'We can pretend we're in Portugal.'

The cab driver raises his eyes to look at us in the mirror. We stare at each other for an uneasy moment. Clarissa laughs. 'It *is* Portugal. At least for a few more years.'

In Macao they've started to send the statues home. Everywhere there are empty pedestals. In Lisbon a man dreamed of children removing the statues' eyes, drowning colourless marbles in thin rivers. And so they sent other men to bring them home, wrapped in cotton like the dead. They didn't own the land anymore, but they still owned the stories and the statues and the bones.

In a small church on Macao's island of Coloane is a box which holds the bones of St Francis Xavier. It sits on a shelf next to the remains of a group of martyred sixteenth century Japanese Catholics. Not all of the saint's bones are here, just the slender humerus of each arm. The rest of St Francis is scattered in various splinters and fragments throughout the world. There are locks of hair in Nagasaki and in the Indian state of Goa, and the intricate joints of the little finger in a velvet-lined casket in Rome. The skull sits in a chapel in a forgotten Portuguese village in Malacca where brown children and goats run through the narrow streets.

When they came for the statues and the chest of bones, they walked, the men from Lisbon, up the hillside to the old seminary of São José. The house sits on high ground above the Praia Grande and when the front and back doors hang open you can see all the way through to the hills beyond. That's how it was the day the Portuguese men came, a square of light framing a distant picture of green hillside dotted with crumbling white stone. A long, empty corridor and a maze of peeling rooms. And in the courtyard, the last priest in the colony, his white cassock trailing in the dust.

Manuel Teixeira came to convert China. They all did, St Francis, the priests from Rome, all of them. They came for the settlers and the savages and for the children. And then, after all the years, they were ordered home. Home to cities they could hardly remember, these men who had grown old in the harshness of the Chinese sun.

He would not go, Father Manuel told the men from Portugal over plates of black olives and small glasses of green wine. He would stay here, in the colony, in the dusty sun and the tired heat, in these, the last years of his life. Yes, he would die here, at São José, on this piece of rock that he had loved and hated in equal measure. He would stay here with the peasants and they would bury him on the hillside.

He gazed at them, these European men sweating in the oriental sun. They could have the statues, he told them. Yes, take the statues, it didn't matter anymore, but not the bones. St Francis's bones belonged to China, to this island. He rose slowly and stood by the door, staring out at the bright band of sky and the slope of the hills. No, he could not let them take the bones.

Watching the old priest they saw, the men from Lisbon, how old he was, how stained and worn his cassock, how dark ridges of dirt filled the cracks in his bare heels. They saw him there and they shifted uncomfortably as he dismissed them with a gesture of his old cracked hand, a gesture which only later appeared to them to take the form of the sign of the cross. They filed, the Portuguese, slowly down the hill path and away from the crumbling seminary.

In a sheaf of church records in a Lisbon office, in a section marked 'Blessed Relics', there is a word next to the entry for the bones of St Francis Xavier which reads 'irrecoverable'.

The hotel is a white villa overlooking the water. The Grand Colonial. Drooping wisteria climbs up one of the walls and there are frangipani trees in the courtyard. In the foyer a dark woman is playing a piano, her fingers trilling the high notes easily.

I place my hand against a pillar. The marble is cool and smooth against my skin.

Our room looks out over the harbour. A boy in a stiff uniform pulls back the drapes and the light spills into the room. There are deck chairs on the terrace. Clarissa splashes gin into chilled glasses and we sit and look out at the garden, the climbing jasmine and the blue of the water beyond.

'I always wanted to come here with a lover,' she says, hitching her dress up above her knees and closing her eyes. 'But now look at me. I'm fit, fat and nearly fifty. I think the time for lovers has passed.'

Dusk in Macao is clear and blue. In the gardens fireflies trace arcs of light. Clarissa is talking about her marriage. 'I married Geoffrey when I was twenty-six. I don't know what I did before then,' she laughs. 'Just had affairs I think.'

Night always comes swiftly here, the sky darkening and

the insects piping up. From the garden we can see the shore stretching away, a long line of winking lights. The waiters place mosquito coils around the pool and they glow in the darkness. The man at the next table is smoking a cigar and the smell drifts towards us.

We take off our shoes and sit on the pool steps, the water calm and tepid around our ankles.

'The thing about marriage,' Clarissa says, 'is that it's like a kind of trophy. You win it and you think you're safe, that it will protect you. But after the fucking stops, it's mostly just boredom and abandonment.' She smiles at me. 'I can only say all this now because I'm a woman of a certain age.'

It's late and the night has grown cool. I tuck my feet up under my skirt. I used to do that when I was a child. Pull my dress over my knees and fold myself up in it. Sometimes I'd hear the sickening tear of stitches if I stretched the cotton too far.

Later, when we are drinking red wine from glass tumblers back in our room, Clarissa leans back in her chair and looks at me. 'That husband of yours,' she says slowly.

Once I saw Joseph and Clarissa talking together at a party. He was speaking in a light, rapid voice and I couldn't make out the words. Then I heard her say, 'Yes, but all those great spires and cathedrals have grown out of some human need.' Joseph stared at her and then he said, 'You mean human weakness.'

'What do you think I should do?' I ask her.

'I'm not the one to ask,' she says. 'Look at me. Forced by love to become pathetic.'

'You're not pathetic.'

She smiles and passes me another cup full of wine.

Long after all of this I will remember the early morning sun over the Kowloon Gardens. The pure, clear skin of morning. Straight monsoon rain on the harbour. These are the images of the country where the people in this story live. All the lives lived in the colony, the relationships that bind people to a particular setting.

This morning I opened a book looking for a particular line of poetry and found an inscription. From a husband to his wife. *For my beloved wife*, he had written. Is this the thread that binds me to him? This proof that once, at least, we wanted the same things.

I sleep and in my dreams I am moving over water, surging

above silver lakes and through the plain of reeds. Here is the green river and the flooded fields and the straight grey reach of the road. There are lighted squares on the Peak. The low window of the Rays' bedroom is yellow against the thickness of the evening. Inside Clarissa is crying, holding a glass between shaky hands and telling her husband with the intensity of desperation that he must stop, that she can't bear it anymore. There is an abstract print on the wall above the bed and her husband is staring at the painting, as if he might find an answer in the twisted skeins of line and colour.

And here is a bookshop, dim and shaded. Behind a dust-streaked window is an old man and a bird in a cage. He is sitting at a table, staring at the outline of petals caught between two pages.

The night is still with the hot mist of August. The fog is thick, it sustains me, carries me. The body is like a streak of light across the bottom of a dark photographer's plate. My fingers brush the lights of the city, the sides of the buildings, the tops of the trees in the Kowloon Gardens.

In the winter Ada began to be sick in the mornings. She has heard the women talk about this dry-mouthed queasiness, this lucid weariness. In the mornings she lies open-eyed in bed and listens to the servants' voices echoing in the hallway. She holds her hands against the still-smooth surface of her stomach and imagines the baby growing inside her like a tiny seedling. She will take this child back to Russia and her mother's friends will kiss the baby's small face and exclaim over her and admire her. There will be the coil of steam from the samovar, the warmth of the dacha, the winter glimmer of hoar frost. This child will replace what she has lost.

Her pregnancy awakened some new spark of life in Ada.

When Victor was away at his office she opened his heavy leather atlas to the map of the world and traced out a route with her finger. She knew that ships left Shanghai for London. Across the blue patches of ocean, all the way to England, then across more water and into the vast reaches of Europe. Her country was pale green and so large that it made all the other nations look like tiny patches of colour. 'Russia,' she murmured to the child inside her at night when her husband was asleep.

She had found a German man who would buy jewellery from her. She took a pair of diamond earrings, a gold chain and an emerald brooch to his room above an alleyway in the Jewish quarter. He had been a jeweller in Cologne and he squinted at the stones through a narrow glass. She pressed the notes he gave her between the pages of one of her books. Her other jewels she sewed carefully into the hem of her winter coat.

Her store of money began to grow. Sometimes when Victor left money scattered across his office desk she would take a note. Never so much that he would notice, or think to raise an alarm. She began to keep back some of the money he gave her to take to her old friends Chaim and Naima Hakham. Every few weeks she would tell Victor that she was going to visit them and he would give her an envelope for them. On the walk to the Jewish quarter she would open the envelope and slip half the money inside her dress.

This was the deception that made her feel ill, this withholding of money from those she knew had greater need of it than she did. But there was no other way, she told herself, she had no other access to Victor's money. This pilfering was the only way she could save herself and her child. Besides, the Hakhams had visas to America, they would soon be leaving for a better life.

Curled up in her chair by the fire, her ankles tucked under her, she feels the baby turn inside her, a foot racing up against her ribs. She gasps and Victor Kadoorie puts his hand on the top of her head. 'Rest up my, dear,' he says, kissing her lightly on the forehead as he leaves for his office. The English doctor has already expressed grave doubts to him. With her small pelvis and delicate health it was bound to be a tough birth, he had told Victor after a measure of scotch. Keep her in bed and feed her up, he said, clapping a hand awkwardly on his shoulder.

One morning at the end of winter, Ada walked down to the harbour with Naima Hakham and asked her to buy her a passage on the next ship to London. Naima thought she was mad. Why did Ada want to go back to the very place she had been so lucky to escape from? Did she have any idea what she was giving up, how foolish she was being? And the child? But Ada pressed the money into her hand and begged her with a kind of desperation. She would die anyway, she said, if she couldn't go home.

That night she slipped the steamer ticket into the small case she had hidden in one of the empty bedrooms at Marble Hall. In two weeks she would be on a ship again, she would have a country again. The baby slipped around inside her like some small sea creature and she smiled to herself.

How does love end? Sometimes I think that the most terrible stories are the ones that are lived by ordinary people every day. The ones that are never written down.

I think that perhaps love ended when Joseph stopped looking at me. He stared as if he could see right through me and yet not see me at all. He stopped meeting my eyes. I didn't know what I had done to make him take his gaze away from me.

When we made love he would close his eyes. I would lie beneath him, with my open-eyed love, and look at the dark shapes of his eyelids. My husband, safe within his solitude.

I tried to explain to him then, about the importance of eyes. In all the drawing primers, first and always first, comes the eye. It is the first thing painters learn, I told him. The utmost pains have to be taken with the depiction of the eye. Every line, and the relationships between them, speaks of character, of the sway of the passions. A painted eye was no glassy-eyed staring, it was the beginning of art. It was the initiation into the mystery of the craft and an emblem of its purpose.

I spoke about the careful mixing of paint. Amateurs paint the white of the eye with unmixed lead white and their eyes have an unnatural opaque cast. The masters know that you have to add a minute quantity of black. In the same way a pupil could never be painted dead black but tinged with brown umber, a dark iris touched with verdigris. Something as simple as the tiny catchlights on the pupil could make a face sorrowful or merry, angry or lustful.

Rembrandt knew about the importance of eyes, I tell Joseph. They sometimes appear on the copper plates of his etchings, floating free of the faces they are supposed to inhabit. It was only when he came to a true crisis of representation that he refused to depict eyes. Faced with painting his own self in all its complexity he gave his portrait gaping black holes instead of eyes. You can still see them, they lie flat and lifeless against the face. Rembrandt enjoyed changing his face with every etching but in this depiction his face is a closed book. He has no eyes.

When I tell him this, Joseph is silent for a long time. He

looks at me with something like distaste. 'The reason you'll never make a good art historian, my dear, is that you mix the facts up with fantasy.'

I hate it when he calls me *my dear*. It makes me feel too tired to fight him, too tired to try and explain myself to him.

Now he's really enjoying himself. 'I don't think you even know any more where the line is. You're so full of bullshit.'

I don't know where his anger comes from. It makes me want to look down at my shoes. I tell him that every history is partly invented, that all we're doing is retelling stories.

'You would think that. That's why you're so bloody unpopular in the department. Because you keep giving them creative diatribes when they want facts.'

It's true. I wasn't popular in the department. But not because I couldn't separate the fiction from the facts. It was because I still believed that the weighty substance of the world could be transferred to a canvas. That someone like Rembrandt could still speak across the centuries to those for whom art might be more than a quest for the new and the shocking.

In Hong Kong, in the muddy light, my sleeping husband looks like one of Rembrandt's imperfect angels. There are blue lines under his eyes and his skin looks faintly florid. He wakes, shakes his head hazily, gropes for his watch. 'Shit Maya, why the hell didn't you wake me up?'

The morning light filters through the gaps in the blinds

and falls in shafts across his face. He frowns as he buttons his shirt. He has lost weight, grown leaner, I think, as I lie in bed watching him.

He leans against the windowsill. His shoulders and hips are more prominent, more angular and the line of his jaw seems sharper to me. Before, I might have learnt this about the body in other ways. It seems strange to me that there was a time when I knew every line and slope of his body, that my fingers could trace over every curve and hollow with ease and familiarity. There have been days this summer when all that has been alive in me is my desire for him to come back to me. But I cannot alter him, cannot change him with the force of my will.

Stein's disappearance has unbalanced him. His desert world, with its absence of political or human contours, has been shattered and he doesn't know what other world to return to. He never speaks to me about any of this. I get up and go over to him and put my hand on his shoulder. Once this place belonged to me.

'It's too hot, Maya,' he says, slipping away from me. He walks to the little kitchen at the end of the hall and turns on the radio. They are talking about typhoons.

'I'll be late tonight.'

'I could come and meet you for dinner.'

There are places we could go. There are restaurants in Lan Kwai Fong, there is the gilt and thick linen of the Peninsula Hotel, the lights of the Island-side cafes. But I have already made my mistake. I say it too tentatively to be a question or an invitation so it is easy for him to refuse.

He kisses my forehead as he leaves. It is a kiss without passion, the imprint of a kiss. Just the shapes of lips on skin.

The June days leading up to the Handover are hot and brooding. It rains every afternoon and the rivers are swollen and green. Fruit lies rotting where it falls and swarms of flies hum in the thick air. There are short spells when the sky clears between storms but for most of the day the city languishes under a stagnant mist. In the afternoons the square is silent and empty.

In the heat I start to think of home. When I think of Australia it is always the colours of the sea and the shrieking call of parrots in the pine trees above the shore. From the window I watch Joseph in the courtyard, talking to a colleague. He's running his hand through his hair, a pile of papers held to his chest. Angry words pass between the men.

The Chinese man turns and walks away across the courtyard.

Joseph has begun to come home in the afternoons. He drifts into the kitchen and stares into the fridge. We have both grown very good at eating on our feet. A handful of cashews or a soft pear. There are no meals across a table.

He stands with his hands in his pockets, his back to me, waiting for the kettle to boil.

I lie on the couch, reading. If I don't open my mouth it is only because there is too much to say. He stands over me, holding his cup between his hands, not saying anything, just watching. There's a sharp smell to the air, as if something's burning.

There's no news of Stein, no trace. Joseph looks condemned, full of sorrow. I start taking walks in the afternoon, even though the heat is almost unbearable, just to get away from him. The flat is too small for grief.

I ask Ken Tiger about Joseph.

'He's in trouble, your husband. He'll have to leave Hong Kong very soon. Things are different now, no-one can afford to offend the Chinese. He and Stein have made a lot of people angry.'

'I didn't realise he was so important.'

'He's doing things that could have serious consequences. He doesn't understand how they are here.'

'What did they do to Stein?'

Ken Tiger is silent for a long time. Finally he says, 'I don't know.'

'What will happen to Joseph?'

'Everyone's toeing the line now. Waiting to see what happens after June thirtieth. The university won't want to make trouble. They'll get orders to dismiss him, you can be sure of that.'

I can't believe that it has come to this. 'But what about his research? He won't leave.'

'There are certain things,' Ken Tiger speaks carefully, 'which are not suggestions.'

I stare into the shaft of light that falls across the room, across the table and onto the old man. His face is obliterated by the shifting light and he seems strange and ethereal, like a picture I once saw of an Egyptian priest whose face shone with the light of God before he died.

I fold my arms on the table and rest my head on them. Ken Tiger puts a hand tentatively on my shoulder.

'It is a strange time. Almost like the end of a world,' he says.

'Yes.'

The end of a world. I have clung too tightly to a world that is not my own. Ken Tiger and Ada and Victor and Clarissa and Joseph. I have spent all these months here trying to pin them down. Have I become only a prism that refracts their stories, their lives?

In Ada's Shanghai, there were rumours of trouble in the north and the whole city was restless. The communists were coming. At Marble Hall, steamer trunks lay half-packed in the hallways. Victor had made arrangements to move to Hong Kong. A house had already been bought on the Peak.

In the confusion, Ada made her own preparations. She grew bold and slipped handfuls of notes out of Victor's wallet. He was too preoccupied to notice. Her small case lay under her bed and she sat with her hands folded over her protruding belly.

The day Ada was to board her ship for Russia, all of Shanghai was seized by panic. The communists had swallowed up whole towns just beyond the edge of the city.

They were in a maelstrom. Ada plaited her hair tightly and put on her travelling dress as the servants bustled around her. Somehow she had to keep herself alert, keep her mind clear for the journey ahead.

Then Victor was standing over her, taking her arm. 'Get in the car Ada, we're taking a plane to Hong Kong.' She recoiled as if her husband had struck her, holding a hand to shield her face. Then she felt a light pain pass over her and the world began to disintegrate. She saw her husband's face looming above hers and felt herself fall sideways, blood pouring down her legs.

On the parquet floor of Marble Hall Victor Kadoorie knelt down beside his wife. He placed his hand gently against her neck, searching for a pulse. His face close to hers, he is conscious of her beauty, the fineness of her face.

The car was already waiting outside. He wrapped his coat around her and lifted her in his arms and walked out of the house, through the darkness and away from their life in Shanghai.

'You must take me home,' Ada whispers in the aeroplane, trying to talk through her pain, 'to Russia.' Her hands clutch at Victor's shirt. She is drenched with sweat, her hair plastered to her forehead. She smells yeasty and damp. 'Victor, please!'

Victor speaks formally to her, his voice loud even against

the drone of the engine. 'Listen Ada, you are not going to Russia. Do you understand? You are not going home. Ever. There is nothing to go back to.'

For a moment she looks at him as if he is the bitterest enemy. Her hands flap at him in rage, her voice is guttural with grief until he yells out her name. 'Ada! Enough!'

Silently she stares up at her husband. Her pupils seems huge to him.

'I love you very much Ada.'

'Yes.'

She falls asleep as the plane grinds down the runway into Hong Kong.

I've seen the house on the Peak where Victor Kadoorie brought Ada. It stands in the middle of a great grove of azaleas. The air is fresh and bloom-scented up here and the house is edged by covered terraces. On one side passionfruit vines have grown over the lattice and there's a sloping garden full of ferns. Water trickles from a stone fountain.

Something in Ada had blown away, torn to shreds in the wake of that terrible flight from Shanghai. In Hong Kong she never spoke of the lost child or of going home. She sat in her high room and stared out at the hard, enamelled blue sky.

The house was airy and light, with windows that faced straight out across the mountain. Standing on the terrace, Victor could see all the way down to the glassy sea below.

'Who'd have thought we'd be living on a mountain top?' he says to Ada, trying for cheeriness. She is sitting at the table eating a piece of toast that has been placed before her. She stares back at him from a place too far for him to reach, then pushes back her chair and turns and walks out of the room. He can hear her footsteps on the tiles.

He told himself that it was just the shock of losing the baby. That the grief would be temporary, that in time she would return to herself. On the way down to his new office on the harbour he sits on the Peak tram and remembers their first days of lovemaking, when she would draw him to her with such passion. He thinks of her pale face beneath him, her eyes always closed, the rise and fall of her small chest. He doesn't know any more, if he ever knew, who his wife is.

In the early morning the sun glints off the harbour. He is struck by how hard and bright the light is here, how different to the muted shadowiness of Shanghai. Jostling his way through the crowds at the docks, the rich aroma of some kind of spice wafting through the air, Victor wonders if this city could ever have been a new beginning for them. A light easterly wind blows against his face and across the water the new buildings seem luminous in the sunlight.

In those first months in Hong Kong Victor became easier with Ada, more indulgent. He loved this new city with its thrust of commerce and its clear light. It made him hopeful. He wanted to impress his wife with this new world, with his place in it. In the evenings she lets him climb into her bed and lie swathed in the sheets with her. 'Ada,' he whispers urgently. When he moves above her she stares beyond his shoulder at the folds of the mosquito net which falls like a bridal veil around them. Her bones feel light, as if they were full of air. She begins to feel a humming in them.

He asks her to come down to the harbour with him. His new office has a little shaded deck, he tells her. He'll put a chair there and she can sit and look out at the docks while he works. The fresh air will be good for her.

On the Peak tram she is quiet but she looks out the window as he points out the nine hills of Kowloon to her, the new bank building, the Chinese graves tumbling down the mountain towards the sea. She allows him to lead her along the narrow path through the docks, her hand light and trembling in his.

Sitting above the docks, a parasol resting against her shoulder, Ada feels completely engulfed and erased. She feels that everything is missing from her body, that her bones are full of air. People swarm around her and she cannot understand a word they are saying. She cannot remember her own language, it has become a series of hieroglyphs, her country a dimly remembered invention.

Ken Tiger pushes the food around on his plate. He is quiet and introspective. I wonder when this shift happened in our friendship, when we began to move towards these intimacies, this shared understanding.

'I could have saved her and I didn't,' he says quietly, looking down. Outside the rain has stopped. I wait, not sure what he wants me to say.

'I saw her there on the docks.' He rubs his jaw. 'I had not seen her for more than a year. Our life together was over. We had both retreated. The communists were preparing for war. I was supposed to be packing up the business, moving everything to Hong Kong.

'I had heard about the baby, I had people who would tell me things about her. I thought that perhaps I was a curse on her. I heard that she was with Victor in Hong Kong.

'So I left Shanghai. Maybe I could have stayed, could have negotiated something with the communists. There are always party cadres who will turn a blind eye for a bit of money. But my life in that city was over.

'That day on the docks. I had heard that she accompanied her husband down to the harbour. I went there just to look at her. She was sitting there with a book in her hands. But it was upside down. As if she had some idea of what she was supposed to be but she couldn't quite manage it. It was upside down.

'I walked up to her and I could see that her face was completely blank. Even her eyes had changed. I said her name and she looked up. And then she said very politely, "Can I help you sir?"

'I should have tried to make her remember. I should have taken her away right then. But I turned and walked away.'

He looks up at me. 'I believe, to this day, that I helped to kill her.'

In a tiny article in one of the newspapers is the story of Ada's death. Just a few lines circling vaguely around the events of that night.

She walks along the path to the docks, her coat trailing on

the ground behind her. The harbour is almost empty at this hour but she imagines she sees eyes watching her. She pauses, looking out at the ships and the lights across the harbour. She has left no note for her husband. Patches of moonlight shine on the water. There's a fisherman upriver, too far away to see her. She stands very close to the edge of the water.

For a moment it feels like just another engulfing; just another embrace. But then the water takes her, the sudden icy swirl of it bearing down on her until there is nothing, just the ripple and flow of the harbour.

There are only four days until the Handover ceremony. Hong Kong is flooded with people from all over the world, come to see the last day of the last colony. There are hundreds of foreign dignitaries, Margaret Thatcher in a summer suit, Lauren Hutton, the King of Tonga. He's so enormous, the Tongan king, that the hotel had to order a special bed made of reinforced iron.

Ken Tiger is not interested in the Handover. He stopped being interested in the political world a long time ago, he told me.

In the heat you have to walk slowly, trailing past the shops, past the signs and the storefronts piled up upon one another like stacks of boxes. The clamour and the closeness of the crowds, the carts, the smell of fish; it's like a market.

There is one man who is always lounging in the same doorway. He has no fingers. On the street they say he lost them in a bet, but it's not true, Ken Tiger told me, there was no bet. He lost them because he loved a prostitute, a 'phoenix'. He would wait for her, outside the club, and look stricken when she walked by, laughing up into a rich white face. You're not allowed to love a phoenix, says Ken Tiger, and they made sure he remembered it.

It seems that you always have to suffer for love, just like in the stories.

There's a tour group blocking the sidewalk, clustered around a slim Chinese girl in a blue suit. She's reading from a page of notes. 'The Fragrant Harbour, as it's known … one of the brightest jewels in the British colonial crown …' They'll have to change the text after Monday. The tour group is restless, it's too hot. They want to be sitting in one of the air-conditioned Chinese restaurants by the harbour.

Further up the crowds have jammed to a halt. There's been an accident. A noodle cart tipped over on the road in front of the dented nose of a taxi. There's a mass of noodles, *lo mein*, spread out over the road, and soda cans rolling away from the overturned cart. A man is shouting in Cantonese, waving his hands angrily.

Ken Tiger's shop is closed, the door locked. I peer through

the dust-streaked glass. The nightingale is hanging in its cage by the window. It flutters its wings then is still again.

I sit at one of the tables on the square and think about the old man. I had imagined that the telling of a life might render it solid, transcribable. But it's not so. In the end, all you are left with are stories. Outlines you have to fill in yourself.

I don't know what Ken Tiger's love came from. Passion, obsession? He closed the door to her because he thought it would be easier not to see her and yet her face is the only thing he's seen all these years. I wonder if he could have been happy with a pretty Chinese wife who would pour his tea and bear him strong sons. With someone who could have loved him in a simple, straightforward way.

I don't know when it is that love stops being the thing we seek and becomes instead what enslaves us.

Ken Tiger never appeared that day in his bookshop. The next day too, the shop is closed. I sit for a long time in the square, waiting to see if he will appear but there is nothing, only the clanging of the hawkers' carts. The mahjong ladies are moving their ivory tiles across the tables. They have slipped their feet from their straw thongs and they hold cups of cold chrysanthemum tea. A yellow dog is sleeping in the full sun beside them. Over the square a Union Jack hangs limply in the stillness of the afternoon.

I ask the women at the mahjong table if they have seen

Ken Tiger. They stare at me blankly then confer in a rapid hum.

'He no come here.'

'Do you have any idea what happened to him? Where he might be?'

They stare at me and shrug. If they know they're not saying.

People in stories disappear. Hong Kong is full of disappearances. Aurel Stein disappeared. People go missing all the time. Sometimes their stories are in the papers, sometimes they're not.

It's violently hot and the sky is full of rain. Clarissa and I go down to the harbour to see the *Britannia* sail into Hong Kong waters. The Royal yacht, sent from England to take the English home. The air is completely still and I can feel beads of sweat trickling down my back. There might be a typhoon. A typhoon would ruin everything. The outdoor ceremony, the farewell fireworks.

I like a pretty ship. The *Britannia*'s sails are billowing like white tablecloths caught by a wind. The sailors on the deck are in their tropical whites too. They look very stark and clean against the dark blue of the hull. They're flying the Union Jack and the crowd bursts into applause, though in a few days they'll be folding up all their flags and sending them home. They've already taken the bronze crown off the wall of the General Post Office and the Queen's head has come off the coins. They're using bauhinias now.

My mother had bauhinias in her garden. We used to call them butterfly flowers. I remember the feel of the petals between the fingers. Light and soft, like a butterfly's wing.

There are other ships in the harbour too. There's a big military launch moored close to land. It's the floating head-quarters for the British forces during their last week in command. On another supply ship they're busy loading all the ammunition that the British kept in their bunkers. I don't know why they needed so many cases of bullets. Just in case, I suppose.

There are only a few soldiers left now, Clarissa tells me. Just to tidy up, switch off the lights, take down the flags. They have to be out of the colony by three-thirty the morning after the Handover.

'Just think,' Clarissa whispers, 'all those Chinese troops lined up on the other side of the border. Ready to march in.'

I think about Joseph, wonder whether he's here watching this too. Last night I came home to find him sitting at the table staring into the empty glass in his hand.

'Been out with your communist buddy have you?' he said nastily. 'Some people might call that disloyalty.'

'He isn't a communist.'

'It doesn't matter. They're all the same, the bloody Chinese. Pitiless, brutal. They look out for themselves and god help anyone who gets in their way.'

'Joseph. Of all of them, Ken's probably on your side.'

'No-one is on *my side*, as you so quaintly put it, Maya.'

I stand behind him and lean forward into him, my face pressed into his shoulder. I can feel his breathing. 'Joseph.' He doesn't move. After a few moments he gets to his feet and sweeps past me into the bedroom. I hear his feet along the tiny hallway and the closing of the door.

I say goodbye to Clarissa at the harbour and go to look for Ken Tiger. He lives in a place called the Walled City. I've never been there but I have his address, scribbled in the flyleaf of a book he has lent me.

I'm looking for high stone walls. In my imagination the Walled City is like a fortress, thick with bricks and guards. But the City has no walls. The Japanese bulldozed them years ago to build another runway for the airport. There are no walls and the entrance is just a gap between two grimy-looking food stalls.

It is almost dark by the time I find Ken Tiger's neighbourhood. The streets are strangely dim, not one welcoming light, not one candle flame. I have no idea where he is, whether he is alive or dead. A cat weaves across the path in front of me.

His house is a narrow stone building. There's no light at

the window. I knock at the door and wait but there is no answer, no scuff of feet or answering call. I lift the latch and push the door open, running my hand across the wall for the light switch.

The first thing I see is her picture. It's a sepia print, like the old portraits on the walls of the Hong Kong Club, but she's not sitting decorously like the ladies in the portraits. She's sitting on a bed, leaning back on her hands. Her face is tilted downwards so that her eyes look up at the photographer. Even in the faded brown tones I can see that she's very beautiful. The sun is on her and her hair sits around her face like the glowing haloes of the saints. Ada. I say her name to myself. Her small, perfect name.

The room is small and plain. There's a wooden table with one chair, a bookshelf, some pots and pans lined up above a tiny stove. There's another door that must lead to the bedroom.

They say you can feel death in a room but it's not true. There's no special smell to it, just the musty closeness of a small room, the faint scent of damp clay. Ken Tiger is there on the bed. Eyes closed, arms crossed neatly over his chest. It's as if he knew this was coming. I stand at the end of the bed, staring down at him as if I'd come to look in on a sleeping child.

I wonder how different his life would have been if Ada could have loved him in the way that he loved her, if her eyes hadn't always been fixed on some other place. A homeland, a dream. What if, licking the sticky crumbs of lotus cake from her fingers, she had told him that she would come away with him.

I don't know. All I know is the story I have.

Walking away from the Walled City I'm thinking about a room with windowsills so low you can see all the way out to the sea. In the breeze the white curtains move against the windows like sails. In the corner there's an old chest made from dark wood, Chinese, and there are rows and rows of tiny drawers with silver handles. I don't know what people would have kept in such a chest. Herbs, medicines, jewels perhaps. I've used it for letters, newspaper stories I've cut out, scraps of paper.

In the room there's a wide bed and a desk by the window. Sitting at the desk you can see the dark shapes of pine trees and beyond them, a square of blue. There's a pot of tea on the desk, some blank pages, a good pen.

As I'm walking back towards the university, the sky looks very low and close. On the harbour the water darkens like mirrors. Whole families live on the junks there. It's like a floating city. In the heat you can see people sleeping under the awnings on the decks. On one there's a small child tied by the waist to a pole. They fasten their children to keep them from tumbling overboard, Clarissa told me.

I like the idea of being clasped firmly around the waist, of being held back from falling.

Just as I reach the apartment it begins to rain. Huge drops sound like hail and the sky looks very dark behind the line of buildings. The courtyard is empty. Then there is the loud wail of the typhoon siren.

Typhoons come down quickly in the summer. It's the winds that are dangerous. Everywhere there are typhoon advisory bulletins telling you what to do when the storms blow in. They tell you to secure loose objects, lock the windows and doors, fasten bars. It's as if, with careful preparations, you might lock out the gale.

They've worried for days that the rains will break on the day of the Handover, that the ceremony will be washed away in gusts of wind and the fireworks will fizzle damply. Tomorrow Prince Charles and the governor will make their speeches under black umbrellas. The Union Jack will be soaking wet when they fold it up. The Chinese troops will march in the rain. The *Britannia* will be lost in a curtain of rain as it sails out of Hong Kong harbour.

I sit with my elbows on the table. The room is very hot and close. Soon the glass in the windows starts to rattle and the lights flicker and go out and I wait in the half-darkness.

A gesture of yours, Joseph, that made me love you. At a party somewhere, years ago, I was standing across the room and I saw you bend down next to a small boy and listen to him as gravely as a judge. Your eyes downcast, nodding slowly at his excited stutter of speech. Your serious face.

I'll always remember the final moment of turning away. The minute I stepped out of his life. I remember everything. The dark sky, the windows of the apartment shaking faintly in the wind, the threat of thunder.

And Joseph. At first I thought that he had injured himself, that he was in pain, his hands clasped to his head. Then I saw that that it was grief. He sank to his knees on the lino floor, slamming his fist against the ground, his face twisted in weeping.

'They've killed Stein. The bastards.'

I can hear him breathing hard, see the real horror in his face. Behind his closed eyes he is seeing the bloated body pulled out of the water, the blue pallor of the face, the brown stain of the wound.

'After everything. After everything we've done here. Years spent in that fucking desert. And these savages …' His whole body is shuddering.

'What am I going to do, Maya?'

I look at his earnest, tear-damp face. Couldn't I get up and put the kettle on, cook some dinner? Why shouldn't we sit at the table smiling at each other in a warm haze of cooking smells, talk about what we're going to do, make plans? Couldn't I console him, tell him that it's not the end of the world, there are other universities, other jobs, other research? I could smile, be kind, pour coffee, let him lie in my arms. I am, after all, his wife.

He's waiting, waiting for his faithful wife to help him.

'There's nothing I can say. It's too late.'

He gapes up at me. I think about how unattractive he looks with swollen eyes, how he needs a shave. Behind him I notice how the paint's lifting from the place above the sink. I want my own kitchen. My rows of glazed plates glowing in the morning sun, my mother's silver coffee pot on the stove, the window looking out over the garden.

I slip my feet into shoes, pick up my string bag and close the door on my husband's bewildered face.

In the early morning the sky is the colour of dust. It hangs low with rain. I walk north, past the square, the gardens, the empty bookshop.

I've got a good coat with a hood for the rain. This morning I took Ken Tiger's nightingale up to the aviary in the Kowloon Gardens. They were happy to take it. It's a good life for a bird there, with all that greenery. I've got my notebook and Ada Lang's picture slipped between the pages of a book. I've got a green Chinese teapot Ken Tiger gave me. It will go well among my Mexican plates in the kitchen of the house by the sea.

I pull my coat around me and look out at the harbour. I'm not waiting for a ship but there's a voyage to come.

In the end we all want to go home.

The rain starts. It's strong and fine. I stand watching the harbour with its seething life, its heavy smells of incense, of summer rain, of escape. The early sun on the buildings, shining. A flaming shield. The rain ending and disappearing from the sky. The clarity that replaces it, pure, like an Australian sky.

In my dreams Ada Lang is standing on the deck of a ship, alone, the wind blowing her wild hair around her face. She's being carried out along the river's length, to the place where it turns into a landless ocean. Horns sound, a wind blows. The dock is full of life and beyond it the city rises up in hazy mountains but she doesn't see it. Her face is turned towards the sea, towards the map she's about to sail into. The ship is on course, ocean-bound. For a long time its dark shape can be seen then slowly, slowly it's swallowed up by the curve of the sea.

Acknowledgements

I would like to thank the Eleanor Dark Foundation for a Varuna Writers' Fellowship during which much of this book was written; the Dorset Writers' Colony in Vermont for generously offering me writing space; and the Fellowship of Australian Writers (WA) for a place in their mentorship program.

Many people have provided perceptive comments and advice on this work and in particular I would like to thank Peter Bishop, Brenda Walker, Chris McLeod, Mark Macleod, Frederic Tuten, Linsey Abrams and Louise Crawford.

I would like to thank my editor Janet Blagg for her intelligence and sensitivity and for helping me discover Ada Lang. Thank you also to all the staff at Fremantle Press for their warmth and support.

Thanks to Lynn Vernon and Edward Ma for sharing their Hong Kong stories with me; Michele Crawford for her generosity and enthusiasm; Annette Allain and Janet McCann for giving me a space to write in New York; and my father for his endless support.

I would like to thank Lucia Russett, Trish Gough, Elizabeth Lopez and Dietra Gamar, who each offered so much to me at the time this book was written.

Book Club notes

For a full version of the Book Club notes, including an
interview with the author, please visit
http://www.fremantlepress.com.au.

Book club discussion questions

1. This is a story in which the very idea of stories is important, from the first sentence, 'My husband told me a story about buildings before we came here.' How much information does this sentence convey at first reading, and then after you have finished the book?

2. Maya loves stories. She finds academic investigations unsatisfying and likes to fill in the gaps with her own imaginings. But who are her stories really for? What is it about the gaps that she feels so compelled to fill them with story? See the conclusion to the story of Maya's Spanish filmmaker friend on page 153: 'She had narrated herself more successfully than I ever could.'

3. What makes Maya follow Ken Tiger? What is it about Ada that fascinates her?

4. The gradual and scarcely acknowledged loss of love between Maya and Joseph seems to be parallelled in Ada and Ken's more graphic story. The author seems to be saying that you can't truthfully know anything more about

Book club discussion questions continued ...

humans and their relationships than can be shown in images; that to fill in more would be to take advantage of the poetic licence of story telling. What do you think? Is it possible to portray people's stories truthfully in more than images or outlines?

5. Various marriages, friendships and other relationships are revealed in the book: Maya and Joseph; Joseph and Stein; Ken and Du; Ken and Ada; Ada and Victor; Clarissa and Geoffrey; Gideon and Hannah. Where is love to be found?

6. How does the Chinese landscape of the novel – Hong Kong, Shanghai and the Taklamakan Desert – reflect the inner lives of its inhabitants? Why do you think that the author has chosen China as the setting for her story? What significance do other landscapes, like Western Australia and New England, hold for the story and its characters?

7. If Joseph were to reflect on his relationship with Maya how might he tell the story?

8. There are many examples of cultural dislocation – the Chinese, the Filipina maids, the ex-pats in Hong Kong, Vietnamese refugees, missionaries in China, the exodus of Russian Jews to Shanghai. Is the ex-pat community in Hong Kong qualitatively different from the other migrant communities described? If so, how, and why?

Book club discussion questions continued ...

9. Maya creates her our own cultural milieu in domestic space with her possessions and decorations, whereas Joseph's office is 'very small and bare.' (p. 127) What does this say about them and their relationship? Would it be relevant to describe it as cross-cultural?

10. Who is Maya? She's a modern woman, an intellectual and a writer, yet she seems remarkably passive. What is happening to her in Hong Kong? What, too, of Ada Lang's passivity?

11. Cups and pots of tea crop up several times through the book. What do you think the author is doing with this recurrent theme? What other images recur?

12. Lines from a Mahmoud Darwish poem reproduced on the back cover provide the book's title: *Where should we go after the last frontiers/ Where should the birds fly after the last sky?* Why do you think the author chose these lines?

13. Do you have photographs or remembered images that distil for you the sense of a relationship or a time in your life? Are there photographs that misrepresent the truth?

14. Why has the book designer used an image of the birdcage on the front cover? Why is the bird no longer in the cage?

Praise for *The Last Sky*

The Last Sky, *set against great social and political upheavals, is a beautiful and exotic story of relationships with many layers. Nelson writes effortlessly and her work will be worth watching.* – readings.com.au

... for those who enjoy beautiful writing and an assured tone and mood, The Last Sky *has much to offer.* – Booksellcr+Publisher

I found Alice Nelson's writing to show echoes of other Perth writers, such as Gail Jones and Brenda Walker. She shares their clear-eyed yet discursive style and their careful, learned use of beautiful language. It will be fascinating to see what she comes up with next. – Canberra Times

... a quite stunning achievement for a first novel ... This author is clearly a major new talent and one to watch for in the future. – Westerly

Nelson's prose is written with poetic cadences and scattered with philosophic musing. Her subtle nuances in language and character interaction speak volumes of her grasp of the human psyche. – Australian Jewish News